Mr. Palomar

BOOKS BY ITALO CALVINO

Italo Calvino

Mr. Palomar

Translated from the Italian by William Weaver

A HARVEST BOOK
A HELEN AND KURT WOLFF BOOK
HARCOURT, INC.
ORLANDO AUSTIN NEW YORK SAN DIEGO TORONTO LONDON

www.HarcourtBooks.com

Library of Congress Cataloging-in-Publication Data
Calvino, Italo.
Mr. Palomar.
Translation of Palomar.
"A Helen and Kurt Wolff book."
Includes index.
I. Title.   II. Title: Mister Palomar.
PQ4809.A45P313   1985
853¢.914   85-5490
ISBN 978-0-15-162835-3
ISBN 978-0-15-662780-1 (Harvest pb)

Designed by Michael Farmer
Printed in the United States of America
X W V U T S R Q

Mr. Palomar

Mr. Palomar's
Vacation

MR. PALOMAR
ON THE BEACH

Reading a wave

The sea is barely wrinkled, and little waves strike the sandy shore. Mr. Palomar is standing on the shore, looking at a wave. Not that he is lost in contemplation of the waves. He is not lost, because he is quite aware of what he is doing: he wants to look at a wave and he is looking at it. He is not contemplating, because for contemplation you need the right temperament, the right mood, and the right combination of exterior circumstances; and though Mr. Palomar has nothing against contemplation in principle, none of these three conditions applies to him. Finally, it is not "the waves" that he means to look at, but just one individual wave: in his desire to avoid vague sensations, he establishes for his every action a limited and precise object.

Mr. Palomar sees a wave rise in the distance, grow, approach, change form and color, fold over itself, break, vanish, and flow again. At this point he could convince himself that he has concluded the operation he had set out to achieve, and he could go away. But isolating one wave is not easy, separating it from the wave immediately following, which seems to push it and at times overtakes it and sweeps it away; and it is no easier to separate that one wave from the preceding wave, which seems to drag it toward the shore, unless it turns against the following wave, as if to arrest it. Then, if you consider the breadth of the wave, parallel to the shore, it is hard to decide where the advancing front extends regularly and where it is separated and segmented into independent waves, distinguished by their speed, shape, force, direction.

In other words, you cannot observe a wave without bearing in mind the complex features that concur in shaping it and the other, equally complex ones that the wave itself originates. These aspects vary constantly, so each wave is different from another wave, even if not immediately adjacent or successive; in other words, there are some forms and sequences that are repeated, though irregularly distributed in space and time. Since what Mr. Palomar means to do at this moment is simply *see* a wave—that is, to perceive all its simultaneous components without overlooking any of them—his gaze will dwell on the movement of the wave that strikes the shore until it can record aspects not previously perceived; as soon as he notices that the images are being repeated, he will know he has seen everything he wanted to see and he will be able to stop.

A nervous man who lives in a frenzied and congested world, Mr. Palomar tends to reduce his relations with the outside world; and, to defend himself against the general neurasthenia, he tries to keep his sensations under control insofar as possible.

The hump of the advancing wave rises more at one point than at any other, and it is here that it becomes hemmed in white. If this occurs at some distance from the shore, there is time for the foam to fold over upon itself and vanish again, as if swallowed, and at the same moment invade the whole, but this time emerging again from below, like a white carpet rising from the bank to welcome the wave that is arriving. But just when you expect that wave to roll over the carpet, you realize it is no longer wave but only carpet, and this also rapidly disappears, to become a glinting of wet sand that quickly withdraws, as if driven back by the expansion of the dry, opaque sand that moves its jagged edge forward.

At the same time, the indentations in the brow of the wave must be considered, where it splits into two wings, one stretching toward the shore from right to left and the other from left to right, and the departure point or the destination of their divergence or convergence is this negative tip, which follows the advance of the wings but is always held back, subject to their alternate overlapping until another wave, a stronger wave, overtakes it, with the same problem of divergence-convergence, and then a wave stronger still, which resolves the knot by shattering it.

Taking the pattern of the waves as model, the beach thrusts into the water some faintly hinted points, prolonged in submerged sandy shoals, shaped and destroyed by the currents at every tide. Mr. Palomar has chosen one of these low tongues of sand as his observation point, because the waves strike it on either side, obliquely, and, overrunning the half-submerged surface, they meet their opposites. So, to understand the composition of a wave, you have to consider these opposing thrusts, which are to some extent counterbalanced and to some extent added together, to produce a general shattering of thrusts and counterthrusts in the usual spreading of foam.

Mr. Palomar now tries to limit his field of observation; if he bears in mind a square zone of, say, ten meters of shore by ten meters of sea, he can carry out an inventory of all the wave movements that are repeated with varying frequency within a given time interval. The hard thing is to fix the boundaries of this zone, because if, for example, he considers as the side farthest from him the outstanding line of an advancing wave, as this line approaches him and rises it hides from his eyes everything behind it, and thus the space under examination is overturned and at the same time crushed.

In any case, Mr. Palomar does not lose heart and at each moment he thinks he has managed to see everything to be seen from his observation point, but then something always crops up that he had not borne in mind. If it were not for his impatience to reach a complete, definitive conclusion of his visual operation, looking at waves would be a very restful exercise for him and could save him from neurasthenia, heart attack, and gastric ulcer. And it could perhaps be the key to mastering the world's complexity by reducing it to its simplest mechanism.

But every attempt to define this model must take into account a long wave that is arriving in a direction perpendicular to the breakers and parallel to the shore, creating the flow of a constant, barely surfacing crest. The shifts of the waves that ruffle toward the shore do not disturb the steady impulse of this compact crest that slices them at a right angle, and there is no knowing where it comes from or where it then goes. Perhaps it is a breath of east wind that stirs the sea's surface against the deep drive that comes from the mass of water far out to sea, but this wave born of air, in passing, receives also the oblique thrusts from the water's depth and redirects them, straightening them in its own direction and bearing them along. And so the wave continues to grow and gain strength until the clash with contrary waves gradually dulls it and makes it disappear, or else twists it until it is confused in one of the many dynasties of oblique waves slammed against the shore.

Concentrating the attention on one aspect makes it leap into the foreground and occupy the square, just as, with certain drawings, you have only to close your eyes and when you open them the perspective has changed. Now, in the overlapping of crests moving in various directions, the general pattern seems broken down into sections that rise and vanish. In addition, the reflux of every wave also has a power of its own that hinders the oncoming waves. And if you concentrate your attention on these backward thrusts, it seems that the true movement is the one that begins from the shore and goes out to sea.

Is this perhaps the real result that Mr. Palomar is about to achieve? To make the waves run in the opposite direction, to overturn time, to perceive the true substance of the world beyond sensory and mental habits? No, he feels a slight dizziness, but it goes no further than that. The stubbornness that drives the waves toward the shore wins the match: in fact, the waves have swelled considerably. Is the wind about to change? It would be disastrous if the image that Mr. Palomar has succeeded painstakingly in putting together were to shatter and be lost. Only if he manages to bear all the aspects in mind at once can he begin the second phase of the operation: extending this knowledge to the entire universe.

It would suffice not to lose patience, as he soon does. Mr. Palomar goes off along the beach, tense and nervous as when he came, and even more unsure about everything.

The naked bosom

Mr. Palomar is walking along a lonely beach. He encounters few bathers. One young woman is lying on the sand taking the sun, her bosom bared. Palomar, discreet by nature, looks away at the horizon of the sea. He knows that in such circumstances, at the approach of a strange man, women often cover themselves hastily, and this does not seem right to him: because it is a nuisance for the woman peacefully sunbathing, and because the passing man feels he is an intruder, and because the taboo against nudity is implicitly confirmed; because half-respected conventions spread insecurity and incoherence of behavior rather than freedom and frankness.

And so, as soon as he sees in the distance the outline of the bronze-pink cloud of a naked female torso, he quickly turns his head in such a way that the trajectory of his gaze remains suspended in the void and guarantees his civil respect for the invisible frontier that surrounds people.

But—he thinks as he proceeds and resumes, the moment the horizon is clear, the free movement of his eyeballs—in acting like this, I display a refusal to see;

or, in other words, I am finally reinforcing the convention that declares illicit any sight of the breast; that is to say, I create a kind of mental brassière suspended between my eyes and that bosom, which, from the flash that reached the edge of my visual field, seemed to me fresh and pleasing to the eye. In other words, my not looking presupposes that I am thinking of that nakedness, worrying about it; and this is basically an indiscreet and reactionary attitude.

Returning from his stroll, Palomar again passes that bather, and this time he keeps his eyes fixed straight ahead, so that his gaze touches with impartial uniformity the foam of the retreating waves, the boats pulled up on shore, the great bath towel spread out on the sand, the swelling moon of lighter skin with the dark halo of the nipple, the outline of the coast in the haze, gray against the sky.

There—he reflects, pleased with himself, as he continues on his way—I have succeeded in having the bosom completely absorbed by the landscape, so that my gaze counted no more than the gaze of a seagull or a hake.

But is this really the right way to act?—he reflects further. Or does it not mean flattening the human person to the level of things, considering it an object, and, worse still, considering as object that which in the person is the specific attribute of the female sex? Am I not perhaps perpetuating the old habit of male superiority, hardened over the years into a habitual insolence?

He turns and retraces his steps. Now, in allowing his gaze to run over the beach with neutral objectivity, he arranges it so that, once the woman's bosom enters his field of vision, a break is noticeable, a shift, almost a darting glance. That glance goes on to graze the taut skin, withdraws, as if appreciating with a slight start the different consistency of the view and the special value it acquires, and for a moment the glance hovers in mid-air, making a curve that accompanies the swell of the breast from a certain distance, elusively but also protectively, and then runs on as if nothing had happened.

In this way I believe my position is made quite clear—Palomar thinks—with no possible misunderstandings. But couldn't this grazing of his eyes finally be taken for an attitude of superiority, an underestimation of what a breast is and means, as if putting it aside, on the margin, or in parentheses? So, I am relegating the bosom again to the semidarkness where centuries of sexomaniacal puritanism and of desire considered sin have kept it. . . .

This interpretation runs counter to Palomar's best intentions, for though he belongs to a human generation for whom nudity of the female bosom was associated with the idea of amorous intimacy, still he hails approvingly this change in customs, both for what it signifies as the reflection of a more broad-minded society and because this sight in particular is pleasing to him. It is this detached encouragement that he would like to be able to express with his gaze.

He does an about-face. With firm steps he walks again toward the woman lying in the sun. Now his gaze, giving the landscape a fickle glance, will linger on the breast with special consideration, but will quickly include it in an impulse of good will and gratitude for the whole, for the sun and the sky, for the bent pines and the dune and the beach and the rocks and the clouds and the seaweed, for the cosmos that rotates around those haloed cusps.

This should be enough to reassure once and for all the solitary sunbather and clear away all perverse assumptions. But the moment he approaches again, she suddenly springs up, covers herself with an impatient huff, and goes off, shrugging in irritation, as if she were avoiding the tiresome insistence of a satyr.

The dead weight of an intolerant tradition prevents anyone's properly understanding the most enlightened intentions, Palomar bitterly concludes.

The sword of the sun

When the sun begins to go down, its reflection takes form on the sea: from the horizon a dazzling patch extends all the way to the shore, composed of countless swaying glints; between one glint and the next, the opaque blue of the sea makes a dark network. The white boats, seen against the light, turn black, lose substance and bulk, as if they were consumed by that splendid speckling.

This is the hour when Mr. Palomar, belated by nature, takes his evening swim. He enters the sea, moves away from the shore; and the sun's reflection becomes a shining sword in the water stretching from the shore to him. Mr. Palomar swims in that sword, or, more precisely, that sword remains always before him; at every stroke of his, it retreats, and never allows him to overtake it. Wherever he stretches out his arms, the sea takes on its opaque evening color, which extends to the shore behind him.

As the sun sinks toward sunset, the incandescent-white reflection acquires gold and copper tones. And wherever Mr. Palomar moves, he remains the vertex of that sharp, gilded triangle; the sword follows him, pointing him out like the hand of a watch whose pivot is the sun.

"This is a special homage the sun pays to me personally," Mr. Palomar is tempted to think, or, rather, the egocentric, megalomaniac ego that dwells in him is tempted to think. But the depressive and self-wounding ego, who dwells with the other in the same container, rebuts: "Everyone with eyes sees the reflection that follows him; illusion of the senses and of the mind holds us all prisoners, always." A third tenant, a more even-handed ego, speaks up: "This means that, no matter what, I belong to the feeling and thinking subjects, capable of establishing a relationship with the sun's rays, and of interpreting and evaluating perceptions and illusions."

Every bather swimming westward at this hour sees the strip of light aimed at him, which then dies out just a bit beyond the spot where his arm extends: each has his *own* reflection, which has that direction only for him and moves with him. On either side of the reflection, the water's blue is darker. "Is that the only non-illusory datum, common to all: darkness?" Mr. Palomar wonders. But the sword is imposed equally on the eye of each swimmer; there is no avoiding it. "Is what we have in common precisely what is given to each of us as something exclusively his?"

The sailboards slide over the water, cutting with side-long swerves the land wind that springs up at this hour. Erect figures hold the boom with arms extended like archers', competing for the air that snaps the canvas. When they cross the reflection, in the midst of the gold that enshrouds them the colors of the sail are muted and the outline of opaque bodies seems to enter the night.

"All this is happening not on the sea, not in the sun," the swimmer Palomar thinks, "but inside my head, in the circuits between eyes and brain. I am swimming in my mind; this sword of light exists only there; and this is precisely what attracts me. This is my element, the only one I can know in some way."

But he also thinks, "I cannot reach that sword: always there ahead, it cannot be inside me and, at the same time, something inside which I am swimming; if I see it I remain outside it, and it remains outside."

His strokes have become weary and hesitant; you would think that all his reasoning, rather than increasing his pleasure in swimming in the reflection, is spoiling it for him, making him feel it as a limitation, or a guilt, or a condemnation. And also a responsibility he cannot escape: the sword exists only because he is there; and if he were to go away, if all the swimmers and craft were to return to the shore, or simply turn their backs on the sun, where would the sword end? In the disintegrating world the thing he would like to save is the most fragile: that sea-bridge between his eyes and the sinking sun. Mr. Palomar no longer feels like swimming; he is cold. But he goes on: now he is obliged to stay in the water until the sun has disappeared.

Then he thinks, "If I see and think and swim the reflection, it is because at the other extreme there is the sun, which casts its rays. Only the origin of what is matters: something that my gaze cannot confront except in an attenuated form, as in this sunset. All the rest is reflection among reflections, me included."

The ghost of a sail passes; the shadow of the mast flows among the luminous scales. "Without the wind this trap put together with plastic joints, human bones and tendons, nylon sheets, would not stand up; it is the wind that makes it a craft that seems endowed with an end and a purpose of its own; it is only the wind that knows where the surf and the surfer are heading," he thinks. What a relief it would be if he could manage to cancel his partial and doubting ego in the certitude of a principle from which everything is derived! A single, absolute principle from which actions and forms are derived? Or else a certain number of distinct principles, lines of force that intersect, giving a form to the world as it appears, unique, instant by instant?

". . . the wind and, obviously, the sea, the mass of water that supports the floating and shifting solid bodies, like me and the sailboard," Mr. Palomar thinks, in a dead-man's float.

His upside-down gaze now contemplates the straying clouds and the hills clouded with woods. His ego is also turned upside down in the elements: the celestial fire, the racing air, the water-cradle and the earth-support. Can this be nature? But nothing of what he sees exists in nature: the sun does not set, the sea does not have this color, the shapes are not those that the light casts on his retina. With unnatural movements of his limbs, he is floating among phantoms; human forms in unnatural positions shift their weight to exploit not the wind but the geometrical abstraction of an angle made by wind and the tilting of an artificial device, and thus they glide over the smooth skin of the sea. Does nature not exist?

The swimming ego of Mr. Palomar is immersed in a disembodied world, intersections of force fields, vectorial diagrams, bands of position lines that converge, diverge, break up. But inside him there remains one point in which everything exists in another way, like a lump, like a clot, like a blockage: the sensation that you are here but could not be here, in a world that could not be but is.

An intrusive wave troubles the smooth sea; a motorboat bursts forth and speeds off, spilling fuel and skipping on its flat belly. In greasy, multicolored glints the skin of oil spreads out, rippling in the water; a material consistency can be doubted in the glint of the sun, but not in this trace of the physical presence of man, who scatters excess fuel in his wake, detritus of combustion, residues that cannot be assimilated, mixing and multiplying the life and death around him.

"This is my habitat," Palomar thinks. "Here there is no question of accepting or rejecting, because I can exist only here, within it." But if the fate of life on earth were already sealed? If the race toward death were to become stronger than any possibility of rescue?

The wave flows, a solitary breaker, until it crashes on the shore; and where there seemed to be only sand, gravel, seaweed, and minute shells, the withdrawal of the water now reveals a margin of beach dotted with cans, peanuts, condoms, dead fish, plastic bottles, broken clogs, syringes, twigs black with oil.

Lifted also by the motorboat's wave, swept off by the tide of residue, Mr. Palomar suddenly feels like flotsam amid flotsam, a corpse rolling on the garbage-beaches of the cemetery-continents. If no eye except the glassy eye of the dead were to open again on the surface of the terraqueous globe, the sword would not gleam any more.

When you come to think of it, such a situation is not new: for millions of centuries the sun's rays rested on the water before there were eyes capable of perceiving them.

Mr. Palomar swims under water, surfaces; there is the sword! One day an eye emerged from the sea, and the sword, already there waiting for it, could finally display its fine, sharp tip and its gleaming splendor. They were made for each other, sword and eye: and perhaps it was not the birth of the eye that caused the birth of the sword, but vice versa, because the sword had to have an eye to observe it at its climax.

Mr. Palomar thinks of the world without him: that endless world before his birth, and that far more obscure world after his death; he tries to imagine the world before eyes, any eyes; and a world that tomorrow, through catastrophe or slow corrosion, will be left blind. What happens (happened, will happen) in that world? Promptly an arrow of light sets out from the sun, is reflected in the calm sea, sparkles in the tremolo of the water; and then matter becomes receptive to light, is differentiated into living tissues, and all of a sudden an eye, a multitude of eyes, burgeons, or reburgeons. . . .

Now all the sailboards have been pulled ashore, and the last shivering swimmer—Mr. Palomar by name—also comes out of the water. He has become convinced that the sword will exist even without him: finally he dries himself with a soft towel and goes home.

MR. PALOMAR
IN THE GARDEN

The loves of the tortoises

There are two tortoises on the patio: a male and a female. *Zlak! Zlak!* Their shells strike each other. It is their mating season.

The male pushes the female sideways, all around the edge of the paving. The female seems to resist his attack, or at least she opposes it with inert immobility. The male is smaller and more active; he seems younger. He tries repeatedly to mount her, from behind, but the back of her shell is steep and he slides off.

Now he must have succeeded in achieving the right position: he thrusts with rhythmic, cadenced strokes; at every thrust he emits a kind of gasp, almost a cry. The female has her foreclaws flattened against the ground, enabling her to raise her hind part. The male scratches with his foreclaws on her shell, his neck stuck out, his mouth gaping. The problem with these shells is that there's no way to get a hold; in fact, the claws can find no purchase.

Now she escapes him; he pursues her. Not that she is faster or particularly determined to run away: to restrain her he gives her some little nips on a leg, always the same one. She does not rebel. Every time she stops, the male tries to mount her; but she takes a little step forward and he topples off, slamming his member on the ground. This member is fairly long, hooked in a way that apparently makes it possible for him to reach her even though the thickness of the shells and their awkward positioning separates them. So there is no telling how many of these attacks achieve their purpose or how many fail, or how many are theater, play-acting.

It is summer; the patio is bare, except for one green jasmine in a corner. The courtship consists of making so many turns around the little patch of grass, with pursuits and flights and skirmishing not of the claws but of the shells, which strike in a dull clicking. The female tries to find refuge among the stalks of the jasmine; she believes—or wants to make others believe—that she does this to hide; but actually this is the surest way to remain blocked by the male, held immobile with no avenue of escape. Now he has most likely managed to introduce his member properly; but this time they are both completely still, silent.

The sensations of the pair of mating tortoises are something Mr. Palomar cannot imagine. He observes them with a cold attention, as if they were two machines: two electronic tortoises programmed to mate. What does eros become if there are plates of bone or horny scales in the place of skin? But what we call eros— is it perhaps only a program of our corporeal bodies, more complicated because the memory receives messages from every cell of the skin, from every molecule of our tissues, and multiplies them and combines them with the impulses transmitted by our eyesight and with those aroused by the imagination? The difference lies

only in the number of circuits involved: from our re-
ceptors billions of wires extend, linked with the com-
puter of feelings, conditionings, the ties between one
person and another. . . . Eros is a program that unfolds in the electronic clusters of the mind, but the mind
is also skin: skin touched, seen, remembered. And what
about the tortoises, enclosed in their insensitive casing?
The poverty of their sensorial stimuli perhaps drives them
to a concentrated, intense mental life, leads them to a
crystalline inner awareness. . . . Perhaps the eros of
tortoises obeys absolute spiritual laws, whereas we are
prisoners of a machinery whose functioning remains
unknown to us, prone to clogging up, stalling, explod-
ing in uncontrolled automatisms. . . .

Do the tortoises understand themselves any better?
After about ten minutes of mating, the two shells separate. She ahead, he behind, they resume their circling
of the grass. Now the male remains more distanced;
every now and then he scratches his claw against her
shell, he climbs on her for a little, but without much
conviction. They go back under the jasmine. He gives
her a nip or two on a leg, always in the same place.

The blackbird's whistle

Mr. Palomar is lucky in one respect: he spends the summer in a place where many birds sing. As he sits in a deck chair and "works" (in fact, he is lucky also in another respect: he can say he is working in places and attitudes that would suggest complete repose; or, rather, he suffers this handicap: he feels obliged never to stop working, even when lying under the trees on an August morning), the invisible birds among the boughs around him display a repertory of the most varied manifestations of sound; they enfold him in an acoustic space that is irregular, discontinuous, jagged; but thanks to an equilibrium established among the various sounds, none of which outdoes the others in intensity or frequency, all is woven into a homogeneous texture, held together not by harmony but by lightness and transparency. Until the hour of greatest heat, when the fierce horde of insects asserts its absolute dominion of the vibrations of the air, systematically filling the dimensions of time and space with the deafening and ceaseless hammering of the cicadas.

The birds' song occupies a variable part of Mr. Palomar's auditory attention. At times he ignores it as a

component of the basic silence, at other times he con-
centrates on distinguishing, within it, one song from
another, grouping them into categories of increasing
complexity: punctiform chirps; two-note trills (one note
long, one short); brief vibrato whistling; gurgles, little
cascades of notes that pour down, spin out, then stop;
overlapping twirls of modulation; and so on, to extended warbling.

Mr. Palomar does not arrive at a less generic classification: he is not one of those people who, on hearing
a birdcall, can identify the bird it belongs to. This ig-
norance makes him feel guilty. The new knowledge the
human race is acquiring does not compensate for the
knowledge spread only by direct oral transmission,
which, once lost, cannot be regained or retransmitted:
no book can teach what can be learned only in child-
hood if you lend an alert ear and eye to the song and
flight of birds and if you find someone who knows how
to give them a specific name. Rather than the cultiva-
tion of precise nomenclature and classification, Palomar
had preferred the constant pursuit of a precision in de-
fining the modulating, the shifting, the composite. Today he would make the opposite choice, and, following
the train of thoughts stirred by the birds' singing, he
sees his life as a series of missed opportunities.

Among all the cries of the birds, the blackbird's whistle
stands out, unmistakable for any other. The blackbirds
arrive in the late afternoon; there are two of them, a
couple certainly, perhaps the same couple as last year,
as every year at this season. Each afternoon, hearing a
whistled summons on two notes, like the signal of a
person wishing to announce his arrival, Mr. Palomar

raises his head to look around for whoever is calling him. Then he remembers that this is the blackbirds' hour. He soon glimpses them: they walk on the lawn as if their true vocation were to be earthbound bipeds, and as if they enjoyed establishing analogies with human beings.

The blackbirds' whistle has this special quality: it is identical to a human whistle, the effort of someone not terribly skilled at whistling but with a good reason for whistling, this once, only this once, not intending to continue, a person who does it in a determined but modest and affable tone, calculated to win the indulgence of anyone who hears him.

After a while the whistle is repeated—by the same blackbird or by its mate—but always as if this were the first time it had occurred to him to whistle; if this is a dialogue, each remark is uttered after long reflection. But is it a dialogue, or does each blackbird whistle for itself and not for the other? And, in whichever case, are these questions and answers (to the whistler or to the mate) or are they confirmations of something that is always the same thing (the bird's own presence, his belonging to this species, this sex, this territory)? Perhaps the value of this single word lies in its being repeated by another whistling beak, in its not being forgotten during the interval of silence.

Or else the whole dialogue consists of one saying to the other "I am here," and the length of the pauses adds to the phrase the sense of a "still," as if to say: "I am here still, it is still I." And what if it is in the pause and not in the whistle that the meaning of the message is contained? If it were in the silence that the blackbirds speak to each other? (In this case the whistle would be a punctuation mark, a formula like "over and out.") A silence, apparently the same as another silence, could express a hundred different notions; a whistle could, too, for that matter. To speak to one another by remaining silent, or by whistling, is always possible; the problem is understanding one another. Or perhaps no one can understand anyone: each blackbird believes that he has put into his whistle a meaning fundamental for him, but only he understands it; the other gives him a reply that has no connection with what he said; it is a dialogue between the deaf, a conversation without head or tail.

But is human dialogue really any different? Mrs. Palomar is also in the garden, watering the veronicas. She says, "There they are," a pleonastic utterance (if it assumes that her husband is already looking at the blackbirds), or else (if he has not seen them) incomprehensible, but in any event intended to establish her own priority in the observation of the blackbirds (because, in fact, she was the first to discover them and to point out their habits to her husband) and to underline their unfailing appearance, which she has already reported many times.

"Sssh," Mr. Palomar says, apparently to prevent his wife from frightening them by speaking in a loud voice (useless injunction, because the blackbirds, husband and wife, are by now accustomed to the presence and voices of the Palomars, husband and wife) but actually to contest the wife's precedence, displaying a consideration for the blackbirds far greater than hers.

Then Mrs. Palomar says, "It's dry again, just since yesterday," referring to the earth in the flower bed she is watering, a communication in itself superfluous but meant to show, as she continues speaking and changes the subject, a far greater familiarity and nonchalance with the blackbirds than her husband has. In any case, from these remarks Mr. Palomar derives a general picture of tranquillity, and he is grateful to his wife for it, because if she confirms the fact that for the moment there is nothing more serious for him to bother about, then he can remain absorbed in his work (or pseudo-work or hyperwork). He allows a minute to pass; then he also tries to send a reassuring message, to inform his wife that his work (or infrawork or ultrawork) is proceeding as usual: to this end he emits a series of sighs and grumbles—". . . crooked . . . for all that . . . repeat . . . yes, my foot . . ."—utterances that, taken all together, transmit also the message "I am very busy," in the event that his wife's last remark contained a veiled reproach on the order of "You could also assume some responsibility for watering the garden."

The premise of these verbal exchanges is the idea that a perfect accord between a married pair allows them to understand each other without having to make everything specific and detailed; but this principle is put into practice in very different ways by the two of them: Mrs. Palomar expresses herself with complete sentences, though often allusive or sibylline, to test the promptness of her husband's mental associations and the syntony of his thoughts with hers (a thing that does not always work); Mr. Palomar, on the other hand, from the mists of his inner monologue allows scattered articulate sounds to emerge, confident that, if a complete meaning does not result, at least the chiaroscuro of a mood will.

Mrs. Palomar, instead, refuses to receive these grumbles as talk, and to underline her nonparticipation she says in a low voice, "Sssh! . . . You'll frighten them," applying to her husband the same shushing that he had believed himself entitled to impose on her, and confirming once more her own primacy as far as consideration for the blackbirds goes.

Having scored this point to her advantage, Mrs. Palomar goes off. The blackbirds peck on the lawn and no doubt consider the dialogue of the Palomars the equivalent of their own whistles. We might just as well confine ourselves to whistling, he thinks. Here a prospect that is very promising for Mr. Palomar's thinking opens out; for him the discrepancy between human behavior and the rest of the universe has always been a source of anguish. The equal whistle of man and blackbird now seems to him a bridge thrown over the abyss.

If man were to invest in whistling everything he normally entrusts to words, and if the blackbird were to modulate into his whistling all the unspoken truth of his natural condition, then the first step would be taken toward bridging the gap between . . . between what and what? Nature and culture? Silence and speech? Mr. Palomar always hopes that silence contains something more than language can say. But what if language were really the goal toward which everything in existence tends? Or what if everything that exists were language, and has been since the beginning of time? Here Mr. Palomar is again gripped by anguish.

After having listened carefully to the whistle of the blackbird, he tries to repeat it, as faithfully as he can. A puzzled silence follows, as if his message required careful examination; then an identical whistle re-echoes.

Mr. Palomar does not know if this is a reply to his or the proof that his whistle is so different that the blackbirds are not the least disturbed by it and resume their dialogue as if nothing had happened.

They go on whistling, questioning in their puzzlement, he and the blackbirds.

The infinite lawn

Around Mr. Palomar's house there is a lawn. This is not a place where a lawn should exist naturally: so the lawn is an artificial object, composed from natural objects, namely grasses. The lawn's purpose is to represent nature, and this representation occurs as the substitution, for the nature proper to the area, of a nature in itself natural but artificial for this area. In other words, it costs money. The lawn requires expense and endless labor: to sow it, water it, fertilize it, weed it, mow it.

The lawn is composed of dichondra, darnel, and clover. This mixture, in equal parts, was scattered over the ground at sowing time. The dichondra, dwarfed and creeping, promptly got the upper hand: its carpet of soft little round leaves spreads everywhere, pleasing to the foot and to the eye. But the lawn is given its thickness by the sharp spears of darnel, if they are not too sparse and if you do not allow them to grow too much before cutting them. The clover sprouts irregularly, some clumps here, nothing there, and farther on a whole sea of it; it grows exuberantly until it slumps, because the helix of the leaf becomes top-heavy and bends the tender stalk. The lawn mower attends with deafening shudder to the tonsure; a light odor of fresh hay intoxicates the air; the leveled grass finds again a bristling infancy; but the bite of the blades reveals unevenness, mangy clearings, yellow patches.

To cut its proper figure, the lawn must be a uniform green expanse: an unnatural result that lawns created by nature achieve naturally. Here, observing it point by point, you discover where the whirling jet of the hose cannot reach, and where the water falls constantly and rots the roots, and where the carefully regulated watering fosters weeds.

Mr. Palomar is crouched on the lawn, pulling up weeds. A dandelion clings to the ground with a foundation of jagged leaves, thickly overlapping; if you tug at the stalk, it breaks off in your hand, while the roots are still sunk into the ground. You have to grasp the entire plant with a curving movement of the hand and delicately slip the roots from the earth, even if you have to pull up a bit of sod and some of the lawn's rare blades of grass, half smothered by their aggressive neighbor. Then you must throw the interloper in a place where it cannot put down roots again or scatter seed. When you start pulling up one weed, you immediately see another appear a bit farther on, and another, and still another. In no time that stretch of lawn, so smooth that it seemed to need only a few touches, proves to be a lawless jungle.

Are only weeds left? Worse: the harmful grasses are so thickly interwoven with the good that you cannot just thrust in your hand and pull. A complicity seems to have been established between the sown grasses and the wild ones, a relaxing of the barriers imposed by difference of birth, a tolerance resigned to deterioration. Some spontaneous grasses, in and of themselves, do not look at all maleficent or insidious. Why not admit them to the company of those that rightfully belong to the lawn, integrating them into the community of the cultivated plants? This is the road that leads to forgetting about the "English-style lawn" and falling back on the "rustic lawn," left to its own devices. "Sooner or later we'll have to make up our minds and accept it," Mr. Palomar thinks, but he feels it would be a betrayal of one's code of honor. A chicory, a borage plant spring into his field of vision. He uproots them.

To be sure, pulling up a weed here and there solves nothing. This is how it should be done, he thinks—take a square section of the lawn, one meter by one meter, and eliminate even the slightest presence of anything but clover, darnel, or dichondra. Then move on to another square. No, perhaps not: remain perhaps with the sample square. Count how many blades of grass there are, what species, how thick, how distributed. On the basis of this calculation you would arrive at a statistical knowledge of the lawn, which, once established . . .

But counting the blades of grass is futile: you would never learn their number. A lawn does not have precise boundaries; there is a border where the grass stops growing, but still a few scattered blades sprout farther on, then a thick green clod, then a sparser stretch: are they still part of the lawn, or not? Elsewhere the underbrush enters the lawn: you cannot tell what is lawn and what is bush. But even where there is nothing but grass, you never know at what point you can stop counting: between one little plant and the next there is always a tiny sprouting leaf that barely emerges from the earth, its root a white wisp hardly perceptible; a moment ago it might have been overlooked, but soon it, too, will have to be counted. Meanwhile, two other shoots that just now seemed barely a shade yellowish have definitively withered and must be erased from the count. Then there are the fractions of blades of grass, cut in half, or shorn to the ground, or split along the nervation, the little leaves that have lost one lobe. . . . The decimals, added up, do not make an integer; they remain a minute grassy devastation, in part still alive, in part already pulp, food for other plants, humus. . . .

The lawn is a collection of grasses—this is how the problem must be formulated—that includes a subcollection of cultivated grasses and a subcollection of spontaneous grasses known as weeds; an intersection of the two subcollections is formed by the grasses that have grown spontaneously but belong to the cultivated species and are therefore indistinguishable from them. The two subcollections, in their turn, include various species, each of which is a subcollection; or, rather, it is a collection that includes the subcollection of its own members, which are members also of the lawn and the subcollection of those alien to the lawn. The wind blows; seeds and pollens fly, the relations among the collections are disrupted. . . .

Mr. Palomar has already moved to another train of thought: is "the lawn" what we see, or do we see one grass plus one grass plus one grass . . . ? What we call "seeing the lawn" is only an effect of our coarse and slapdash senses; a collection exists only because it is formed of discrete elements. There is no point in counting them, the number does not matter; what matters is grasping in one glance the individual little plants, one by one, in their individualities and differences. And not only seeing them: thinking them. Instead of thinking "lawn," to think of that stalk with two clover leaves, that lanceolate, slightly humped leaf, that delicate corymb. . . .

Mr. Palomar's mind has wandered, he has stopped pulling up weeds. He no longer thinks of the lawn: he thinks of the universe. He is trying to apply to the universe everything he has thought about the lawn. The universe as regular and ordered cosmos or as chaotic proliferation. The universe perhaps finite but countless, unstable within its borders, which discloses other universes within itself. The universe, collection of celestial bodies, nebulas, fine dust, force fields, intersections of fields, collections of collections . . .

MR. PALOMAR
LOOKS AT THE SKY

Moon in the afternoon

Nobody looks at the moon in the afternoon, and this is the moment when it would most require our attention, since its existence is still in doubt. It is a whitish shadow that surfaces from the intense blue of the sky, charged with solar light; who can assure us that, once again, it will succeed in assuming a form and glow? It is so fragile and pale and slender; only on one side does it begin to assume a distinct outline, like the arc of a sickle, while the rest is all steeped in azure. It is like a transparent wafer, or a half-dissolved pastille; only here the white circle is not dissolving but condensing, collecting itself at the price of gray-bluish patches and shadows that might belong to the moon's geography or might be spillings of the sky that still soak the satellite, porous as a sponge.

In this phase the sky is still something very compact and concrete, and you cannot be sure whether it is from its taut, uninterrupted surface that this round and whitish shape is being detached, its consistency only a bit more solid than the clouds', or whether it is a corrosion of the basic tissue, a rift in the dome, a crevice that opens onto the void behind. The uncertainty is height-

ened by the irregularity of the figure that on one side
is taking shape (where the rays of the setting sun arrive)
and on the other lingers in a kind of penumbra. And
since the border between the two zones is not sharply
defined, the effect is not that of a solid seen in perspective but, rather, of one of those little drawings of the
moon on calendars, where a white outline stands within
a little dark circle. There would be nothing to object to
in this if it were a moon in the first quarter and not a
full, or almost full, moon. This, in fact, is what is being
revealed, gradually, as its contrast with the sky becomes stronger and its circumference is being more distinctly outlined, with only a few dents on the eastern
edge.

It must be said that the sky's blue has veered succes-
sively toward periwinkle, toward violet (the sun's rays
have become red), then dulled toward ashen, and each
time the whiteness of the moon has received an impulse
to emerge more firmly, and inside it, the more luminous part has gained ground, until it now covers the
whole disk. It is as if the phases that the moon passes
through in a month were covered inside this full or gib-
bous moon, in the hours between its rising and its setting, with the difference that the round form remains
more or less in sight. In the midst of the circle the spots
are still there—indeed, their chiaroscuro becomes more
distinct thanks to the luminosity of the rest—but now
there is no doubt that it is the moon that bears them,
like stains or bruises, and they can no longer be taken
for transparencies of the sky's ground, rips in the cloak
of a bodiless ghost-moon.

What remains uncertain, rather, is whether this gain

in evidence and in splendor is due to the slow retreat of the sky, which, as it moves away, sinks deeper and deeper into darkness, or whether, on the contrary, it is the moon that is coming forward, collecting the previously scattered light and depriving the sky of it, concentrating it all in the round mouth of its funnel.

And especially these changes must not make us forget that in the meantime the satellite has been shifting in the sky, proceeding westward and upward. The moon is the most changeable body in the visible universe, and the most regular in its complicated habits: it never fails to show up for an appointment, and you can always wait for it at the appointed spot; but if you leave it in one place, you always find it next in another, and if you recall its face turned in a certain way, you see it has already changed its pose, a little or a lot. In any case, following it steadily, you do not realize that it is imperceptibly eluding you. Only the clouds intervene to create the illusion of a rapid dash and rapid metamorphoses, or, rather, to underline vividly what would otherwise escape the eye.

The cloud dashes; gray at first, it becomes milky and shiny, the sky behind it has turned black, it is night, the stars are lighted, the moon is a great, dazzling mirror that flies. Who would recognize in this moon the one of a few hours ago? Now it is a lake of shininess, spurting rays all around, brimming in the darkness with a halo of cold silver, and flooding with white light the streets of the night walkers.

There is no doubt that what is now beginning is a splendid winter night of full moon. At this point, assured that the moon no longer needs him, Mr. Palomar goes home.

The eye and the planets

When he learns that this year, for the entire month of April, the three "external" planets, visible to the naked eye (even his, nearsighted and astigmatic), are all three "in opposition" and therefore visible for the whole night, Mr. Palomar rushes out onto the terrace.

Because of the full moon, the sky is light. Mars, though close to the great lunar mirror flooded with white light, advances imperiously with its stubborn radiance, its thick, concentrated yellow, so different from all the other yellows of the firmament that it has finally been agreed to call it red, and in moments of inspiration really to see it as red.

Moving your gaze down, continuing eastward an imaginary arc that should link Regulus with Spica (but Spica can hardly be seen), you encounter, quite distinctly, Saturn with its chilly whitish light, and still farther down there is Jupiter, in the moment of its greatest splendor, a vigorous yellow with a hint of green. The stars all around have paled, except Arcturus, which shines with a defiant air, a bit higher to the east.

To enjoy most fully the triple planetary opposition it is necessary to procure a telescope. Mr. Palomar, perhaps because he bears the same name as a famous

observatory, can boast some friendships among astronomers, and he is allowed to put his nose beside the
eyepiece of a 15-centimeter telescope. It is rather small
for scientific research, but compared with his eyeglasses
it makes quite a difference.

For example, in the telescope Mars proves to be a
more perplexed planet than it appears to the naked eye:
it seems to have many things to communicate and can
bring only a small portion of them into focus, as in a
stammered, coughing speech. A scarlet halo protrudes
around the edge; you can try to tuck it in by regulating
the screw, to emphasize the crust of ice of the lower
pole; spots appear and vanish on the surface like clouds
or rents in clouds; one becomes stabilized in the shape
and position of Australia, and Mr. Palomar is convinced that the more clearly he sees that Australia, the
more the lens is focused; but at the same time he realizes that he is losing other shadows of things that he
thought he saw or felt obliged to see.

In other words, it seems to him that if Mars is the
planet about which, ever since the days of Schiaparelli,
so many things have been said, causing alternate illusions and disappointments, this fact coincides with the
difficulty of establishing relations with the planet, as
with a person of difficult character. (Unless the difficulty of character is all on Mr. Palomar's side: he tries
in vain to escape subjectivity by taking refuge among
the celestial bodies.)

Quite the opposite is the relationship he establishes
with Saturn, the most exciting planet to the person
viewing it through a telescope: there it is, very sharp,
white, the outlines of the sphere precise and of the ring;

a faint zebra striping marks the sphere; a darker circumference distinguishes the edge of the ring. This telescope hardly picks up any other details and accentuates the geometrical abstraction of the object; the sense of an extreme difference, rather than diminishing, becomes more prominent now than it is to the naked eye.

It is cheering to think that an object so different from all others, a form that achieves the maximum strangeness with the maximum simplicity and regularity and harmony, is rotating in the sky.

"If the ancients had been able to see it as I see it now," Mr. Palomar thinks, "they would have thought they had projected their gaze into the heaven of Plato's ideas, or in the immaterial space of the postulates of Euclid; but instead, thanks to some misdirection or other, this sight has been granted to me, who fear it is too beautiful to be true, too gratifying to my imaginary universe to belong to the real world. But perhaps it is this same distrust of our senses that prevents us from feeling comfortable in the universe. Perhaps the first rule I must impose on myself is this: stick to what I see."

Now it seems to him that the ring is swaying slightly, or the planet is, within the ring, and both seem to rotate in place. In reality it is Mr. Palomar's head that is swaying as he is forced to twist his neck to fit his gaze into the eyepiece of the telescope; but he takes care not to deny privately this illusion, which coincides with his expectation as it does with natural truth.

Saturn really is like this. Since the Voyager 2 expedition Mr. Palomar has read everything written about the rings: they are made of microscopic particles; they are made of boulders of ice separated by abysses; the divisions between the rings are furrows in which the satellites rotate, sweeping away matter and piling it up at the sides, like sheepdogs running around the flock to keep it compact. He followed the discovery of intertwined rings which were then proved to be simple circles, much thinner; and the discovery of the opaque streaks arranged like the spokes of a wheel, later identified as icy clouds. But the new information does not deny this essential figure, no different from what was first seen by Gian Domenico Cassini in 1676, when he discovered the division between the rings that bears his name.

For the occasion a scrupulous person like Mr. Palomar would naturally have consulted encyclopedias and manuals. Now Saturn, an ever-new object, presents itself to his gaze, renewing the wonder of the first discovery, and prompting the regret that Galileo with his blurred spyglass was able only to conceive a confused idea, of triple body or of sphere with two handles, and when he was coming close to understanding how it was made, his eyesight failed and everything plunged into darkness.

Staring at a luminous body too long tires the vision; Mr. Palomar closes his eyes; he moves on to Jupiter.

In its majestic but not heavy bulk, Jupiter displays two equatorial stripes like a scarf decorated with interwoven embroideries, of a pale bluish green. Effects of immense atmospheric storms are translated into a calm, orderly pattern, an elaborate composure. But the real pomp of this luxurious planet is its glittering satellites, all four now in sight along an oblique line, like a scepter shining with jewels.

Discovered by Galileo, who named them *Medicea sidera*, "Medici stars," rebaptized a little later with Ovidian names—Io, Europa, Ganymede, Callisto—by a Dutch astronomer, Jupiter's little planets seem to cast a final glow of neoplatonic Renaissance, as if unaware that the impassive order of the celestial spheres had dissolved because of the work of their discoverer himself.

A dream of classicality enshrouds Jupiter; gazing at it through the telescope, Mr. Palomar awaits an Olympian transfiguration. But he is unable to keep the image sharp: he has to lower his eyelids for a moment, let the dazzled pupil find again the precise perception of outlines, colors, shadows, but also let the imagination strip away borrowed garments and renounce its show of book learning.

Though it is right for the imagination to come to support weakness of vision, it must be immediate and direct like the gaze that kindles it. What was the first simile that occurred to him, and which he dismissed because it was incongruous? He had seen the planet sway, with its satellites in line like air bubbles rising from the gills of a round fish of the depths, luminescent and striped. . . .

The following night Mr. Palomar goes out on his terrace again, to see the planets with his naked eye. The great difference is that here he is forced to bear in mind the proportions between the planet, the rest of the firmament scattered in dark space on all sides, and himself, watching: something that does not happen if the relation is between the isolated object-planet focused by the lens and himself-subject, in an illusory face-to-face encounter. At the same time he remembers that

detailed image of each planet he saw last night, and tries
to insert it into that minuscule dot of light that pierces
the sky. In this way he hopes that he has truly taken
possession of the planet, or at least of as much of a
planet as an eye can take in.

The contemplation of the stars

When it is a beautiful starry night Mr. Palomar says, "I *must* go and look at the stars." That is exactly what he says—"I *must*"—because he hates waste and believes it is wrong to waste the great quantity of stars that is put at his disposal. He says "I *must*" also because he has little practical knowledge of how you look at the stars, and this simple action always costs him a certain effort.

The first problem is to find a place from which his gaze can move freely over the whole dome of the sky without obstacles and without the invasion of electric light: for example, a lonely beach on a very low coast.

Another necessary condition is to bring along an astronomical chart, without which he would not know what he is looking at; but between times he forgets how to orient it and he has first to devote a half hour to studying it. To decipher the chart in the darkness he must also bring along a flashlight. The frequent checking of sky against chart requires him to turn the light on and off, and in the passages from light to darkness he remains almost blinded and has to readjust his vision every time.

If Mr. Palomar employed a telescope, things would be more complicated in some ways and simplified in others; but for the present, the experience of the sky that interests him is that of the naked eye, like that of ancient navigators and nomad shepherds. Naked eye for him, who is nearsighted, means eyeglasses; and since he has to remove his eyeglasses to study the chart, operations are complicated by this pushing up and lowering of the eyeglasses on his brow, and there is a wait of several seconds before his crystalline lenses can focus the real stars or the printed ones. On the chart the names of the stars are written in black on a blue ground, and he has to hold the flashlight against the paper in order to make them out. When he raises his eyes to the sky, he sees it black, scattered with vague glows; only gradually do the stars become fixed, set in precise patterns, and the more he looks, the more stars he sees emerge.

Furthermore, the celestial charts he has to consult are two, or, rather, four: one, very synthetic, of the sky in that month, which presents separately the Southern Hemisphere and the Northern; and one of the entire firmament, much more detailed, which shows in a long strip the constellations of the whole year for the central part of the sky around the horizon, whereas those of the segment around the Pole Star are included in a separate, circular map. In other words, to locate a star involves the checking of various maps against the vault of the sky, with all the related actions: putting on and taking off eyeglasses, turning the flashlight on and off, unfolding and folding the large chart, losing and finding again the reference points.

Since the last time Mr. Palomar looked at the stars,

weeks or months have gone by; the sky is all changed; the Great Bear (it is August) is stretched out, almost lying down, on the crowns of the trees to the north-west; Arcturus plunges toward the outline of the hill, dragging the entire kite of the Dipper with him; exactly west is Vega, high and solitary; that star over the sea is Altair; and up above is Deneb, which emits a cold ray from its zenith.

Tonight the sky seems far more crowded than any chart. The schematic patterns prove in reality to be more complicated and less distinct; each cluster could contain that triangle or that broken line you are seeking; and each time you look up at a constellation it seems a bit different.

In identifying a constellation, the decisive proof is to see how it answers when you call it. More convincing than the matching of distances and configurations with those marked on the chart is the reply that the luminous dot gives to the name by which it has been called, its promptness in responding to that sound, becoming one with it. For those of us who are ignorant of all mythology, the names of the stars seem incongruous, arbitrary; and yet you could never consider them interchangeable. When the name that Mr. Palomar has found is the right one, he realizes it at once, because it makes the star necessary, gives it a salience it lacked before; on the other hand, if the name is wrong, the star loses it after a few seconds, as if shrugging it off, and you no longer know where it was and who it was.

Several times Mr. Palomar decides that Berenice's Hair (a constellation he loves) is this or that luminous swarm in the direction of Serpentarius, but he does not feel

again the throb he felt on previous occasions on recognizing that object, so sumptuous and yet so light.
Only later does he realize that he cannot find it because
in this season Berenice's Hair cannot be seen.

Much of the sky is streaked with light stripes and
patches; in August the Milky Way assumes a dense
consistency, and you might say it is overflowing its bed;
the dark and the light are so mixed that they prevent
the effect of perspective of a black abyss against whose
empty remoteness the stars stand out, in relief; everything remains on the same plane: glitter and silvery cloud
and shadows.

Is this the exact geometry of the sidereal spaces, which
Mr. Palomar has so often felt the need to turn to, in
order to detach himself from the earth, that place of
superfluous complications and confused approxima-
tions? When he finds himself really in the presence of
the starred sky, everything seems to escape him. Even
that aspect to which he thought himself most sensitive,
the smallness of our world compared with the vast distances, does not emerge directly. The firmament is
something that is up there, you can see that it exists,
but from it you can derive no idea of dimensions or
distance.

If the luminous bodies are filled with uncertainty, the
only solution is to entrust oneself to the darkness, to
the deserted regions of the sky. What can be more
stable than nothingness? And yet we cannot be 100-
percent sure even of nothingness. Where Mr. Palomar
sees a clearing in the firmament, a breach, empty and
black, there he fixes his gaze, as if projecting himself
into it; and then, even there, some brighter grain begins

to form, a little patch or dot; but he cannot be sure if it is really there or if he just seems to see it. Perhaps it is a glow like those you see rotating when you keep your eyes shut (the dark sky is like the obverse of the eyelids, furrowed by phosphenes); perhaps it is a glint from his eyeglasses; but it could also be an unknown star surfacing from the most remote depths.

This observation of the stars transmits an unstable and contradictory knowledge—Palomar thinks—the exact opposite of what the ancients were able to derive from it. Is this because his relationship with the sky is intermittent and agitated rather than a serene habit? If he forced himself to contemplate the constellations night after night and year after year, following their progress, their returns along the curved tracks of the dark vault, he, too, would perhaps gain in the end the notion of a continuing and unchangeable time, separated from the labile and fragmentary time of terrestrial events. But would attention to the celestial revolutions be enough to stamp this imprint on him? Or would not a special inner revolution be necessary, something he could suppose only theoretically, unable to imagine the palpable effects on his emotions and on the rhythms of his mind?

Of the mythical knowledge of the stars he picks up only a weary glimmering; of the scientific knowledge, the echoes popularized by the newspapers. He distrusts what he knows; what he does not know keeps his spirit in a suspended state. Oppressed, insecure, he becomes nervous over the celestial charts, as over railroad timetables when he flips through them in search of a connection.

There, a glowing arrow slices the sky. A meteor?

These are the nights when you sight shooting stars most frequently. But it could also easily be a brightly lighted commercial plane. Mr. Palomar's gaze remains alert, available, released from all certitude.

He has been on the dark beach for an hour, seated on a deck chair, twisting toward the south or toward the north, every now and then turning on the flashlight and holding the charts to his nose, after keeping them spread out on his lap; then, craning his neck backward, he begins the exploration again, setting out from the Pole Star.

Some silent shadows are moving over the sand: a pair of lovers rises from the dune, a night fisherman, a customs man, a boatman. Mr. Palomar hears a whispering. He looks around: a few paces from him a little crowd has gathered, observing his movements like the convulsions of a madman.

Mr. Palomar
in the City

From the terrace

_____

"Shoo! Shoo!" Mr. Palomar rushes onto the terrace to drive away the pigeons, who eat the leaves of the gazania, riddle the succulent plants with their beaks, cling with their claws to the cascade of morning-glories, peck at the blackberries, devour leaf by leaf the parsley planted in the box near the kitchen, dig and scratch in the flowerpots, spilling dirt and baring the roots, as if the sole purpose of their flights were devastation. The doves whose flying once cheered the city's squares have been followed by a degenerate progeny, filthy and infected, neither domestic nor wild, but integrated into the public institutions and, as such, inextinguishable. The sky of Rome has long since fallen under the dominion of the overpopulation of these lumpen-fowl, who make life difficult for every other species of bird in the area and oppress the once free and various kingdom of the air with their monotonous, molting, lead-gray livery.

Trapped between the subterranean hordes of rats and the grievous flight of the pigeons, the ancient city allows itself to be corroded from below and from above, offering no more resistance than it did in the past to the barbarian invasions as if it saw not the assault of external enemies but the darkest, most congenital impulses of its own inner essence.

The city has also another soul—one of the many—that lives on the harmony between old stones and ever-new vegetation, sharing the favors of the sun. Fostering this good environmental attitude or *genius loci*, the Palomar family's terrace, a secret island above the rooftops, dreams of concentrating under its pergola the luxuriance of the gardens of Babylon.

The luxuriance of the terrace corresponds to the desire of each member of the family. For Mrs. Palomar it was natural to extend to the plants the attention she reserved for individual things, chosen and made her own through an inner identification and thus becoming part of a composition with multiple variations, an emblematic collection; but this spiritual dimension is lacking in the other members of the family. In the daughter because youth cannot and should not become fixed on the here but only on the further-on, the over-there; in the husband because he was too late in freeing himself from his youthful impatiences and in understanding (only in theory) that salvation lies solely in applying oneself to the things that are there.

The concerns of the cultivator, for whom what matters is that given plant, that given piece of ground exposed to the sun from this hour to that hour, that given disease of the leaves which must be fought in time with that given treatment, are alien to the mind modeled on the processes of industry, led to make decisions along general lines, according to prototypes. When Mr. Palomar realized how approximate and doomed to error are the criteria of a world where he had thought to find precision and universal norm, he slowly reverted to the direct observation of visible forms; but by then he was the way he was: his connection with things has remained the intermittent and labile tie of one who seems always intent on thinking of something else, though this something else does not exist. His contribution to the burgeoning of the terrace is to run out every now and then to frighten the pigeons—Shoo! Shoo!—waking in himself the atavistic sense of defending the territory.

If birds other than pigeons light on the terrace, instead of driving them away Mr. Palomar welcomes them, closes an eye to any possible damage done by their beaks, considers them the messengers of friendly deities. But these appearances are rare: a patrol of crows occasionally approaches, punctuating the sky with black patches, and spreading (even the language of the gods changes with the centuries) a sense of life and gaiety. Then an occasional blackbird, polite and clever; once a robin; and sparrows in their usual role of anonymous passers-by. Other feathered presences over the city allow themselves to be sighted at a greater distance: the squadrons of migratory birds in autumn, and the acrobatics, in summer, of swallows and house martins. From time to time, white gulls, rowing the air with their long wings, venture over the dry sea of tiles, lost perhaps in following the bends of the river from its mouth, or intent perhaps on a nuptial rite, and their marine cry shrieks among the city noises.

The terrace is on two levels: a loggia or belvedere dominates the hurly-burly of the roofs over which Mr. Palomar casts a bird's-eye glance. He tries to conceive the world as it is seen by birds. Unlike him, birds have the void opening beneath them, but perhaps they never look down, they see only to the side, hovering obliquely on their wings, and their gaze, like his, wherever it turns, encounters nothing but roofs, higher or lower, constructions more or less elevated but so thick that he can move only so far down. That, down below, hemmed in, streets and squares exist, that the true ground is the one at ground level, he knows on the basis of other experiences; at this moment, from what he can see from up here, he would never suspect it.

The true form of the city is in this rise and fall of roofs, old tiles and new, curved and flat, slender or squat chimneys, arbors of reed matting and sheds of corrugated iron, railings, balustrades, little columns supporting pots, metal water tanks, dormers, glass skylights, and, rising above all else, the rigging of TV antennas, straight or crooked, enameled or rusting, in models of successive generations, variously ramified and horned and shielded, but all of them thin as skeletons and disturbing as totems. Separated by irregular and jagged gulfs of emptiness, proletarian terraces with lines for drying laundry and with tomato plants growing in tin cans directly face residential terraces with espaliered plants growing against wooden trellises, garden furniture of white-painted cast iron, awnings; pealing campaniles; façades of public buildings, in profile and full-face; garrets and penthouses, illegal and unpunished constructions; pipe scaffoldings of constructions in progress or left half finished; large windows with curtains, and little WC windows; ocher walls and burnt-sienna walls, walls the color of mold from whose crevices clumps of weeds spill their pendulous foliage; ele-

vator shafts; towers with double and triple mullioned
windows; spires of churches with madonnas; statues of
horses and chariots; great mansions that have decayed
into hovels, hovels restructured into smart bachelor
apartments; and domes that make round outlines against
the sky in every direction and at every distance, as if to
confirm the female, Junoesque essence of the city: white
domes or pink or violet, according to the hour and the
light, veined with nervatures, crowned by lanterns surmounted by other, smaller domes.

Nothing of this can be seen by one who moves on
his feet or his wheels over the city pavements. And,
inversely, from up here you have the impression that
the true crust of the earth is this, uneven but compact,
even if furrowed by gaps whose depth cannot be known,
chasms or pits or craters whose edges seem in perspective to overlap like the scales of a pine cone, and it
never even occurs to you to wonder what is hidden in
their depth, because the panorama of the surface is already so vast and rich and various that it more than
suffices to saturate the mind with information and
meanings.

This is how birds think, or at least this is how Mr.
Palomar thinks, imagining himself a bird. "It is only
after you have come to know the surface of things," he
concludes, "that you can venture to seek what is underneath. But the surface of things is inexhaustible."

The gecko's belly

On the terrace, the gecko has returned, as he does every summer. An exceptional observation point allows Mr. Palomar to see him not from above, as we have always been accustomed to seeing geckos, tree frogs, and lizards, but from below. In the living room of the Palomar home there is a little show-case window and display case that gives onto the terrace; on the shelves of this case a collection of Art Nouveau vases is aligned; in the evening a 75-watt bulb illuminates the objects; a plumbago plant trails its pale-blue flowers from the wall against the outside glass. Every evening, as soon as the light is turned on, the gecko, who lives under the leaves on that wall, moves onto the glass, to the spot where the bulb shines, and remains motionless, like a lizard in the sun. Gnats fly around, also attracted by the light; when a gnat comes within range, the reptile swallows it.

Every evening Mr. Palomar and Mrs. Palomar end up shifting their chairs from the television set, to place them near the glass; from the interior of the room they contemplate the whitish form of the reptile against the dark background. The choice between television and gecko is not always made without some hesitation; each of the two spectacles has some information to offer that the other does not provide. The television ranges over continents gathering luminous impulses that describe the visible face of things; the gecko, on the other hand, represents immobile concentration and the hidden side, the obverse of what is displayed to the eye.

The most extraordinary thing is the claws, actual hands with soft fingers, all pad, which, pressed against the glass, adhere to it with their minuscule suckers: the five fingers stretch out like the petals of little flowers in a childish drawing, and when one claw moves, the fingers close like a flower, only to spread out again and flatten against the glass, making tiny streaks, like fingerprints. At once delicate and strong, these hands seem to contain a potential intelligence, so that if they could only be freed from their task of remaining stuck there to the vertical surface they could acquire the talents of human hands, which are said to have become skilled after they no longer had to cling to boughs or press on the ground.

Bent, the legs seem not so much all knee as all elbow, elastic in order to raise the body. The tail adheres to the glass only along a central strip, from which begin the rings that circle it from one side to the other and make of it a sturdy and well-protected implement; most of the time it is listless, idle, and seems to have no talent or ambition beyond subsidiary support (nothing like the calligraphic agility of lizards' tails); but when called upon, it proves well articulated, ready to react, even expressive.

Of the head, the vibrant, capacious gullet is visible,

and the protruding, lidless eyes at either side. The throat is a limp sack's surface extending from the tip of the chin, hard and all scales like that of an alligator, to the white belly, which, where it presses against the glass, also reveals a grainy, perhaps adhesive speckling.

When a gnat passes close to the gecko's throat, the tongue flicks and engulfs, rapid and supple and prehensile, without shape, capable of assuming whatever shape. In any case, Mr. Palomar is never sure if he has seen it or not seen it. What he surely does see, now, is the gnat inside the reptile's gullet: the belly pressed against the illuminated glass is transparent as if under X-rays; you can follow the shadow of the prey in its course through the viscera that absorb it.

If all material were transparent—the ground that supports us, the envelope that sheathes our body—everything would be seen not as a fluttering of impalpable wings but as an inferno of grinding and ingesting. Perhaps at this moment a god of the nether world situated in the center of the earth with his eye that can pierce granite is watching us from below, following the cycle of living and dying, the lacerated victims dissolving in the bellies of their devourers, until they, in their turn, are swallowed by another belly.

The gecko remains motionless for hours; with a snap of his tongue he gulps down a mosquito or a gnat every now and then; other insects, on the contrary, identical to the first, light unawares a few millimeters from his mouth, and he seems not to perceive them. Is it the vertical pupil of his eyes, separated at the sides of his head, that does not notice? Or does he have criteria of choice and rejection that we do not know? Or are his actions prompted by chance, or by whim?

The segmentation of legs and tail into rings, the speckling of tiny granulous plates on his head and belly give the gecko the appearance of a mechanical device: a highly elaborate machine, its every microscopic detail carefully studied, so that you begin to wonder if all that perfection is not squandered, in view of the limited operations it performs. Or is this perhaps the secret: content to be, does he reduce his doing to the minimum? Can this be his lesson, the opposite of the morality that, in his youth, Mr. Palomar wanted to make his: to strive always to do something a bit beyond one's means?

Now a bewildered nocturnal butterfly comes within range. Will he overlook it? No, he catches this, too. His tongue is transformed into a butterfly net and he pulls it into his mouth. Will it all fit? Will he spit it out? Will he explode? No, the butterfly is there in his throat: it flutters, in a sorry state but still itself, not touched by the insult of chewing teeth; now it passes the narrow limits of the neck; it is a shadow that begins its slow and troubled journey down along a swollen esophagus.

The gecko, emerging from its impassiveness, gasps, shakes its convulsed throat, staggers on legs and tail, twists its belly, subjected to a severe test. Will this be enough for him for tonight? Will he go away? Was this the peak of every desire he yearned to satisfy? Was this the nearly impossible test in which he wanted to prove himself? No, he stays. Perhaps he has fallen asleep. What is sleep like for someone who has eyes without eyelids?

Mr. Palomar is unable to move from there, either. He sits and stares at the gecko. There is no truce on which he can count. Even if he turned the television back on, he would only be extending the contemplation of massacres. The butterfly, fragile Eurydice, sinks slowly into her Hades. A gnat flies, is about to light on the glass. And the gecko's tongue whips out.

The invasion of the starlings

There is something extraordinary to be seen in Rome in this late autumn and it is the sky crammed with birds. Mr. Palomar's terrace is a good observation post; from it his gaze roves over roofs along a broad circle of horizon. Of these birds he knows only what he has heard people saying: they are starlings, which gather by the hundreds of thousands, coming from the north, waiting until it is time for them to leave all together for the coasts of Africa. At night they sleep on the city's trees, and anyone who parks his car on the street along the Tiber is obliged to wash it the next morning from stem to stern.

Where do they go during the day? What function does this prolonged stopover in one city have in the strategy of their migration? What meaning do these immense evening assemblies have for them, this aerial pageant like a parade or the great annual maneuvers? Mr. Palomar has not yet managed to understand. The explanations offered are all a bit dubious, conditioned by hypotheses, wavering among various alternatives; and this is only natural, since these are rumors that pass from mouth to mouth, while even science, which should confirm or deny them, is apparently uncertain, approximate. Things being as they are, then, Mr. Palomar has decided to confine himself to watching, to establishing down to the slightest detail what little he sees, sticking to the immediate ideas that what he sees suggests.

In the violet sunset air he watches a very minute dust surface from one part of the sky, a cloud of flying wings. He realizes that they are thousands and thousands: the dome of the sky is invaded. What had seemed so far a serene and empty immensity proves to be all traversed by very rapid and light presences.

A reassuring sight, the passage of migratory birds is associated in our ancestral memory with the harmonious succession of the seasons; instead, Mr. Palomar feels something akin to apprehension. Can it be because this crowding of the sky reminds us that the balance of nature has been lost? Or is it because our sense of insecurity finds threats of catastrophe everywhere?

When you think of migratory birds, you usually imagine a very orderly and compact flight formation, which furrows the sky in a long host or a right-angled phalanx, like a bird-shape made up of countless birds. This image does not apply to the starlings, or at least not to these autumnal starlings in the Roman sky: this is an airy crowd that seems always about to scatter and disperse, like grains of a powder suspended in a liquid; instead, it thickens constantly as if from an invisible conduit the jet of whirling particles continued, never managing, however, to saturate the solution.

The cloud spreads, blackening with wings outlined more sharply in the sky, a sign that they are approaching. Inside the flock Mr. Palomar can already discern a perspective, for he sees some of the birds already very near, over his head, others far off, others farther still, and he continues discovering more, tinier and puncti-form, for kilometers and kilometers, you would say, attributing to the distances between one and another an almost equal length. But this illusion of regularity is treacherous, because nothing is more difficult to eval-uate than the density of distribution of birds in flight, where the compactness of the flock seems about to darken the sky. There, between one winged animal and the next, chasms of emptiness yawn.

If he lingers for a few moments to observe the ar-rangement of the birds, one in relation to another, Mr. Palomar feels caught in a weft whose continuity ex-tends, uniform and without rents, as if he, too, were part of this moving body composed of hundreds and hundreds of bodies, detached, but together forming a single object, like a cloud or a column of smoke or a jet of water—something, in other words, that even in the fluidity of its substance achieves a formal solidity of its own. But he has only to start following a single bird with his gaze and the disassociation of the ele-ments returns; and the current that he felt transporting him, the network that he felt sustaining him, dissolve; the effect is that of a vertigo that grips him at the pit of the stomach.

This happens, for example, when Mr. Palomar, after having convinced himself that the flock as a whole is flying toward him, directs his gaze to a bird that is, on the contrary, moving away, and from this one to an-other, also moving away but in a different direction; and he soon notices that all the birds that seemed to

him to be approaching are in reality flying off in all
directions, as if he were in the center of an explosion.
But if he simply turns his eyes toward another zone of
the sky, there they are, concentrated over there, in an
increasingly thick and crammed vortex, as when a mag-
net hidden under a sheet of paper attracts iron filings,
making patterns that become darker one moment, lighter
the next, and in the end dissolve and leave on the white
page a speckling of scattered fragments.

Finally a form emerges from the confused flutter of
wings, advances, condenses: it is a circular shape, like
a sphere, a bubble, the balloon-speech of someone who
is thinking of a sky full of birds, an avalanche of wings
that rolls in the air and involves all the birds flying in
the vicinity. This sphere, in the uniform space, represents a special territory, a moving volume within whose
confines—which still dilate and contract like an elastic
surface—the flocks can go on flying, each in its own
direction provided they do not alter the circular shape
of the whole.

At a certain point Mr. Palomar realizes that the number of whirling creatures inside the globe is rapidly increasing, as if a very swift current were decanting there
a new population with the speed of sand in an hour-
glass. It is another gust of starlings that also assumes a
spherical form, spreading out within the preceding form.
But the cohesion of the flock does not seem to resist
beyond certain dimensions: in fact, Mr. Palomar is already observing a dispersion of birds at the edges, or,
rather, real gaps open and begin to deflate the sphere.
He barely has time to notice it before the pattern has
dissolved.

Mr. Palomar's observations on birds succeed one another and multiply at such a pace that Mr. Palomar feels the need to communicate them to his friends. His friends also have something to say on the subject, either because each of them has happened to take some interest in the phenomenon already or else because some interest has been awakened in them after Mr. Palomar has talked to them. It is a subject that can never be considered exhausted, and when one of the friends believes he has seen something new or feels called upon to rectify a previous impression, he seems obliged to telephone the others at once. And so there is a to and fro of messages along the telephone network as the sky is crisscrossed by hosts of birds.

"Have you noticed how they manage to avoid one another even when they are flying closest together, even when their paths intersect? You'd think they had radar."

"That's not so. I've found lots of birds on the pavement, battered or dying or dead. They're the victims of collisions in flight, inevitable when the density is too great."

"I've figured out why they keep flying all together in the evening over this area of the city. They're like planes stacked up over the airport, circling until they get a permission-to-land signal. That's why we see them flying around for such a long time: they're waiting their turn to perch on the trees where they will spend the night."

"I've seen how they act when they light on the trees. They fly around and around in the sky, in a spiral, then one by one they dive very fast toward their chosen tree, then they brake sharply and light on the branch."

"No, aerial traffic jams can't be a problem. Each bird

has a tree that is his, he has his branch and his place on
the branch. He can pick it out from above and he dives."

"Is their eyesight so sharp?"

"Hmph."

The phone calls are never long: Mr. Palomar is impatient to get back to the terrace, as if he were afraid
of missing some decisive turn of events.

Now you would say that the birds occupy only that
portion of the sky that is still struck by the rays of the
setting sun. But taking a better look, you realize that
the condensing and thinning out of the birds unwinds
like a long ribbon, flapping in a zigzag. Where this ribbon curves the flock seems thicker, like a swarm of bees;
where it stretches out, not twisting, there is only a dotting of scattered flights.

Until the last glow vanishes in the sky, and a tide of
darkness rises from the depths of the streets to sub-
merge the archipelago of tiles and domes and terraces
and garrets and loggias and spires; and the suspension
of the black wings of the celestial invaders precipitates
until it is confused with the grievous flight of the stu-
pid, spattering urban pigeons.

MR. PALOMAR
DOES THE SHOPPING

Two pounds of goose fat

The goose fat is shown in glass jars, each containing, as the handwritten label says, "two limbs of plump goose (a leg and a wing), goose fat, salt and pepper. Net weight: two pounds." In the thick, soft whiteness that fills the jars, the clangor of the world is muffled: a dark shadow rises from the bottom and, as in the fog of memories, allows a glimpse of the goose's severed limbs, lost in its fat.

Mr. Palomar is standing in line in a Paris charcuterie. It is the holiday season, but here the throng of customers is usual even at less ceremonial times, because this is one of the good gastronomical shops of the city, miraculously surviving in a neighborhood where the leveling of mass trade, taxes, the low income of the consumers, and now the depression have dismantled the old shops, one by one, replacing them with anonymous supermarkets.

Waiting in line, Mr. Palomar contemplates the jars. He tries to find a place in his memories for cassoulet, a rich stew of meats and beans in which goose fat is an essential ingredient; but neither his palate's memory nor his cultural memory is of any help to him. And yet the name, the sight, the idea attract him, awaken an immediate fantasy not so much of appetite as of eros: from a mountain of goose fat a female figure surfaces, smears white over her rosy skin, and he already imagines himself making his way toward her through those thick avalanches, embracing her, sinking with her.

He dispels this incongruous thought from his mind, raises his eyes to the ceiling bedecked with salamis that hang from the Christmas wreaths like fruit from boughs in the land of Cockaigne. All around, on the marble counters, abundance triumphs in the forms developed by civilization and art. In the slices of game pâté, the pursuits and flights of the moor are fixed forever, sublimated in a tapestry of flavors. The galantines of pheasant are arrayed in gray-pink cylinders surmounted, to certify their origin, by two bird feet like talons that jut from a coat-of-arms or from a Renaissance chest.

Through the gelatine sheaths the thick beauty spots of black truffle stand out, aligned like buttons on a Pierrot's tunic, like the notes of a score, dotting the roseate, variegated beds of pâtés de foie gras, of head cheese, terrines, galantines, fans of salmon, artichoke hearts garnished like trophies. The leading motive of the little truffle discs unifies the variety of substances like the black of dinner jackets at a masked ball, distinguishing the festive dress of the foods.

Gray and opaque and sullen, on the contrary, are the people who make their way among the counters, shunted by salesladies in white, more or less elderly, brusquely efficient. The splendor of the salmon canapés radiant with mayonnaise disappears, swallowed by the dark shopping bags of the customers. Certainly every one of these men and women knows exactly what he wants, heads straight for his objective with a decisiveness admitting no hesitancy; and rapidly he dismantles mountains of vol-au-vents, white puddings, cervelats.

Mr. Palomar would like to catch in their eyes some reflection of those treasures' spell, but the faces and actions are only impatient and hasty, of people concentrated on themselves, nerves taut, each concerned with what he has and what he does not have. Nobody seems to him worthy of the Pantagruelic glory that unfolds in those cases, on the counters. A greed without joy or youth drives them; and yet a deep, atavistic bond exists between them and those foods, their consubstance, flesh of their flesh.

He realizes he is feeling something closely akin to jealousy: he would like the duck and hare pâtés, from their platters, to show they prefer him to the others, recognizing him as the only one deserving of their gifts, those gifts that nature and culture have handed down for millennia and that must not now fall into profane hands! Is not the sacred enthusiasm that he feels pervading him perhaps a sign that he alone is the elect, the one touched by grace, the only one worthy of the deluge of good things brimming from the cornucopia of the world?

He looks around, waiting to hear the vibration of an orchestra of flavors. No, nothing vibrates. All those delicacies stir in him imprecise, blurred memories; his imagination does not instinctively associate flavors with images and names. He asks himself if his gluttony is not chiefly mental, aesthetic, symbolic. Perhaps, for all the sincerity of his love of galantines, galantines do not love him. They sense that his gaze transforms every food into a document of the history of civilization, a museum exhibit.

Mr. Palomar wishes the line would advance more rapidly. He knows that if he spends a few more hours in this shop, he will end up convincing himself that he is the profane one, the alien, the outsider.

The cheese museum

Mr. Palomar is standing in line in a cheese shop, in Paris. He wants to buy certain goat cheeses that are preserved in oil in little transparent containers and spiced with various herbs and condiments. The line of customers moves along a counter where samples of the most unusual and disparate specialties are displayed. This is a shop whose range seems meant to exemplify every conceivable form of dairy product; the very sign, "Spécialités froumagères," with that rare archaic or vernacular adjective, advises that here is guarded the legacy of a knowledge accumulated by a civilization through all its history and geography.

Three or four girls in pink smocks wait on the customers. The moment one of the girls is free, she deals with the first in line and asks him to express his wishes; the customer names or, more often, points, moving about the shop toward the object of his specific and expert appetites.

At that moment the whole line moves forward one place; and the person who till then had been standing beside the "Bleu d'Auvergne" veined with green now finds himself at the level of the "Brin d'amour," whose whiteness holds strands of dried straw stuck to it; the customer contemplating a ball wrapped in leaves can now concentrate on a cube dusted with ash. At each move forward, some customers are inspired by new stimuli and new desires: they may change their minds about what they were about to ask for or may add a new item to the list; and there are also those who never allow themselves to be distracted even for a moment from the objective they are pursuing and every different, fortuitous suggestion serves only to limit, through exclusion, the field of what they stubbornly want.

Mr. Palomar's spirit vacillates between contrasting urges: the one that aims at complete, exhaustive knowledge and could be satisfied only by tasting all the varieties; and the one that tends toward an absolute choice, the identification of the cheese that is his alone, a cheese that certainly exists even if he cannot recognize it (cannot recognize himself in it).

Or else, or else: it is not a matter of choosing the right cheese, but of being chosen. There is a reciprocal relationship between cheese and customer: each cheese awaits its customer, poses so as to attract him, with a firmness or a somewhat haughty graininess, or, on the contrary, by melting in submissive abandon.

There is a hint of complicity hovering in the air: the refinement of the taste buds and especially of the olfactory organs has its moments of weakness, of loss of class, when the cheeses on their platters seem to proffer themselves as if on the divans of a brothel. A perverse grin flickers in the satisfaction of debasing the object of one's own gluttony with lowering nicknames: *crottin*, *boule de moine*, *bouton de culotte*.

This is not the kind of acquaintance that Mr. Palomar is most inclined to pursue; he would be content to establish the simplicity of a direct physical relationship between man and cheese. But since in place of the cheeses he sees names of cheeses, concepts of cheeses, meanings of cheeses, histories of cheeses, contexts of cheeses, psychologies of cheeses, when he does not so much know as sense that behind each of these cheeses there is all that, then his relationship becomes very complicated.

The cheese shop appears to Mr. Palomar the way an encyclopedia looks to an autodidact: he could memorize all the names, venture a classification according to the form—bar of soap, cylinder, dome, ball—according to the consistency—dry, buttery, creamy, veined, firm—according to the alien materials involved in the crust or in the heart—raisins, pepper, walnuts, sesame seeds, herbs, molds—but this would not bring him a step closer to true knowledge, which lies in the experience of the flavors, composed of memory and imagination at once. Only on the basis of this could he establish a scale of preferences and tastes and curiosities and exclusions.

Behind every cheese there is a pasture of a different green under a different sky: meadows caked with salt that the tides of Normandy deposit every evening; meadows scented with aromas in the windy sunlight of Provence; there are different flocks, with their stablings and their transhumances; there are secret processes handed down over the centuries. This shop is a museum: Mr. Palomar, visiting it, feels as he does in the Louvre, behind every displayed object the presence of the civilization that has given it form and takes form from it.

This shop is a dictionary; the language is the system of cheeses as a whole: a language whose morphology records declensions and conjugations in countless variants, and whose lexicon presents an inexhaustible richness of synonyms, idiomatic usages, connotations, and nuances of meaning, as in all languages nourished by the contribution of a hundred dialects. It is a language made up of things; its nomenclature is only an external aspect, instrumental; but for Mr. Palomar, learning a bit of nomenclature still remains the first measure to be taken if he wants to stop for a moment the things that are flowing before his eyes.

From his pocket he takes a notebook and a pen, and begins to write down some names, marking beside each name some feature that will enable him to recall the image to his memory; he tries also to make a synthetic sketch of the shape. He writes *pavé d'Airvault*, and notes "green mold," draws a flat parallelopiped and to one side notes "4 cm. circa"; he writes *St-Maure*, notes "gray granular cylinder with a little shaft inside," and draws it, measuring it at a glance as about "20 cm."; then he writes *Chabicholi* and draws another little cylinder.

"Monsieur! Hoo there! Monsieur!" A young cheese-girl, dressed in pink, is standing in front of him while he is occupied with his notebook. It is his turn, he is next; in the line behind him, everyone is observing his incongruous behavior, heads are being shaken with those half-ironic, half-exasperated looks with which the inhabitants of the big cities consider the ever-increasing number of the mentally retarded wandering about the streets.

The elaborate and greedy order that he intended to

make momentarily slips his mind; he stammers; he falls back on the most obvious, the most banal, the most advertised, as if the automatons of mass civilization were waiting only for this moment of uncertainty on his part in order to seize him again and have him at their mercy.

Marble and blood

The reflections the butcher shop inspires in someone
entering with a shopping bag involve information handed
down for centuries in various branches of learning: ex-
pertise in meats and cuts, the best way of cooking each
piece, the rites that allay remorse at the ending of other
lives in order to sustain one's own. Butchering wisdom
and culinary doctrine belong to the exact sciences, which
can be checked through experimentation, bearing in mind
the habits and techniques that vary from one country
to another; sacrificial practice, on the other hand, is
dominated by uncertainty, and what's more fell into
oblivion centuries ago, but still it weighs obscurely on
the conscience, an unexpressed demand. A reverent de-
votion for everything that concerns meat guides Mr.
Palomar, who is preparing to buy three steaks. Amid
the marble slabs of the butcher shop he stands as if in
a temple, aware that his individual existence and the
culture to which he belongs are conditioned by this place.

The line of customers moves slowly along the high
marble counter, past the shelves and the trays where
the cuts of meat are aligned, each with its name and
price on a tag stuck into it. The vivid red of the beef

precedes the light pink of the veal, the dull red of the
lamb, the dark red of the pork. Vast ribs blaze up, round
tournedos whose thickness is lined by a ribbon of lard,
slender and agile contre-filets, steaks armed with their
invincible bone, massive rolled roasts all lean, chunks
for boiling with layers of fat and of red meat, roasts
waiting for the string that will force them to enfold
themselves. Then the colors fade: veal escalopes, loin
chops, pieces of shoulder and breast, cartilage; and then
we enter the realm of legs and shoulders of lamb; farther
on some white tripe glows, a liver glistens blackly. . . .

Behind the counter, the white-smocked butchers
brandish their cleavers with the trapezoidal blades, their
great knives for slicing and for flaying, saws for severing bones, pounders with which to press the snaky pink
curls into the funnel of the grinding machine. From
hooks hang quartered carcasses to remind you that your
every morsel is part of a being whose living complete-
ness has been arbitrarily torn asunder.

On the wall a chart shows an outline of a steer, like
a map covered with frontier lines that mark off the areas
of consuming interest, involving the entire anatomy of
the animal except only horns and hoofs. The map of
the human habitat is this, no less than the planisphere
of the planet; both are protocols that should sanction
the rights man has attributed to himself, of possession,
division, and consumption without residue of the terrestrial continents and of the loins of the animal body.

It must be said that the man-beef symbiosis has, over
the centuries, achieved an equilibrium (allowing the two
species to continue multiplying), though it is asymmet-
ric (it is true that man takes care of feeding cattle, but

he is not required to give them himself to feed on), and
has guaranteed the flourishing of what is called human
civilization, which at least in part should be called
human-bovine (coinciding in part with the human-ovine
and in smaller part with the human-porcine, depending
on the alternatives of a complicated geography of reli-
gious prohibitions). Mr. Palomar shares in this symbiosis with a clear conscience and full agreement: though
he recognizes in the strung-up carcass of the beef the
person of a disemboweled brother, and in the slash of
the loin chop the wound that mutilates his own flesh,
he knows that he is a carnivore, conditioned by his al-
imentary background to perceive in a butcher shop the
premise of gustatory happiness, to imagine, observing
these reddish slices, the stripes that the flame will leave
on the grilled steaks and the pleasure of the tooth in
severing the browned fiber.

One sentiment does not exclude another: Mr. Palomar's mood as he stands in line in the butcher shop is
at once of restrained joy and of fear, desire and respect,
egoistic concern and universal compassion, the mood
that perhaps others express in prayer.

MR. PALOMAR
AT THE ZOO

The giraffe race

———————

Visiting the Vincennes zoo, Mr. Palomar stops at the giraffes' yard. Every now and then the adult giraffes start running, followed by the baby giraffes; they charge almost to the fence, wheel around, repeat the dash two or three times, then stop. Mr. Palomar never tires of watching the giraffes' race, fascinated by their unharmonious movements. He cannot decide whether they are galloping or trotting, because the stride of their hind legs has nothing in common with that of their forelegs. The forelegs arch loosely to the breast, then unfold to the ground, as if unsure which of numerous articulations they should employ at that given moment. The hind legs, much shorter and stiff, follow in leaps and bounds, somewhat obliquely, as if they were of wood, or crutches stumbling along, but also as if playing, aware of being comical. Meanwhile the outstretched neck sways up and down, like the arm of a crane, with no possible relationship between the movement of the legs and the movement of the neck. The withers also give a jolt, but this is simply the movement of the neck that jerks the rest of the spinal column.

The giraffe seems a mechanism constructed by putting together pieces from heterogeneous machines, though it functions perfectly all the same. Mr. Palomar, as he continues observing the racing giraffes, becomes aware of a complicated harmony that commands that unharmonious trampling, an inner proportion that links the most glaring anatomical disproportions, a natural grace that emerges from those ungraceful movements. The unifying element comes from the spots on the hide, arranged in irregular but homogeneous patterns: they agree, like a precise graphic equivalent, with the animal's segmented movements. The hide should not be considered spotted, but, rather, a black coat whose uniformity is broken by pale veins that open in a lozenge design: an unevenness of pigmentation that preannounces the unevenness of the movements.

At this point Mr. Palomar's little girl, who has long since tired of watching the giraffes, pulls him toward the penguins' cave. Mr. Palomar, in whom penguins inspire anguish, follows her reluctantly and asks himself why he is so interested in giraffes. Perhaps because the world around him moves in an unharmonious way, and he hopes always to find some pattern in it, a constant. Perhaps because he himself feels that his own advance is impelled by uncoordinated movements of the mind, which seem to have nothing to do with one another and are increasingly difficult to fit into any pattern of inner harmony.

The albino gorilla

In the Barcelona zoo there exists the only exemplar known in the world of the great albino ape, a gorilla from equatorial Africa. Mr. Palomar picks his way through the crowd that presses into the animal's building. Beyond a sheet of plate glass, "Copito de Nieve" ("Snowflake," as they call him) is a mountain of flesh and white hide. Seated against a wall, he is taking the sun. The facial mask is a human pink, carved by wrinkles; the chest also reveals a pink and glabrous skin, like that of a human of the white race. Every now and then that face with its enormous features, a sad giant's, turns upon the crowd of visitors beyond the glass, less than a meter away, a slow gaze charged with desolation and patience and boredom, a gaze that expresses all the resignation at being the way he is, sole exemplar in the world of a form not chosen, not loved, all the effort of bearing his own singularity, and the suffering at occupying space and time with his presence so cumbersome and evident.

The glass looks onto an enclosure surrounded by high masonry walls, which give it the appearance of a prison yard, but actually it is the "garden" of the gorilla's house-

cage; from its soil rises a squat leafless tree and an iron
ladder like those in a gymnasium. Farther back in the
yard there is the female, a great black gorilla carrying a
baby in her arms: the whiteness of the coat cannot be
inherited, Copito de Nieve remains the only albino of
all gorillas.

White and motionless, the great ape suggests to
Mr. Palomar's mind an immemorial antiquity, like
mountains or like the pyramids. In reality the animal is
still young, and only the contrast between the pink face
and the short snowy coat that frames it and, especially,
the wrinkles all around the eyes give him the look of
an old man. For the rest, the appearance of Copito de
Nieve shows fewer resemblances to humans than that
of other primates: in place of a nose, the nostrils dig a
double chasm; the hands, hairy and—it would seem—
not very highly articulated, at the end of the very long
and stiff arms, are actually still paws, and the gorilla
uses them as such when he walks, pressing them to the
ground like a quadruped.

Now these arm-paws are pressing a rubber tire against
his chest. In the enormous void of his hours, Copito
de Nieve never abandons the tire. What can this object
be for him? A toy? A fetish? A talisman? Mr. Palomar
feels he understands the gorilla perfectly, his need for
something to hold tight while everything eludes him, a
thing with which to allay the anguish of isolation, of
difference, of the sentence to being always considered a
living phenomenon, not only by the visitors to the zoo
but also by his own females and his children.

The female has an old tire, too, but for her it is an
object of normal use, with which she has a practical

relationship, without problems: she sits in it as if it were an easy chair, sunbathing and delousing her infant. For Copito de Nieve, on the contrary, the contact with the tire seems to be something affective, possessive, and somehow symbolic. From it he can have a glimpse of what for man is the search for an escape from the dismay of living—investing oneself in things, recognizing oneself in signs, transforming the world into a collection of symbols—a first daybreak of culture in the long biological night. To do all this the gorilla has only an old tire, an artifact of human production, alien to him, lacking any symbolic potentiality, naked of meanings, abstract. Looking at it, you would not say that much could be derived from it. And yet what, more than an empty circle, can contain all the symbols you might want to attribute to it? Perhaps identifying himself with it, the gorilla is about to reach, in the depths of silence, the springs from which language burst forth, to establish a flow of relationships between his thoughts and the unyielding, deaf evidence of the facts that determine his life. . . .

Leaving the zoo, Mr. Palomar cannot dispel the image of the albino gorilla from his mind. He tries to talk about him with people he meets, but he cannot make anyone listen. At night, both during the hours of insomnia and during his brief dreams, the great ape continues to appear to him. "Just as the gorilla has his tire, which serves as tangible support for a raving, wordless speech," he thinks, "so I have this image of a great white ape. We all turn in our hands an old, empty tire through which we try to reach some final meaning, which words cannot achieve."

The order squamata

Mr. Palomar would like to know why iguanas attract him. In Paris he goes now and then to visit the reptile house of the Jardin des Plantes; he is never disappointed. What is extraordinary, indeed unique, about the appearance of the iguana in itself is quite clear to him; but he feels there is something more, and he cannot say what it is.

The *Iguana iguana* is covered with a green skin that seems woven from very tiny speckled scales. There is too much of this skin: on the neck, on the legs it forms folds, bags, flounces, like a dress that should adhere to the body and instead sags on all sides. Along the spinal column there is a jagged crest that extends to the tail; the tail also starts out green but in lengthening it fades progressively and becomes divided into alternating light-brown and dark-brown rings. On the scaly green snout, the eye opens and closes, an "evolved" eye, endowed with gaze, attention, sadness, suggesting that another being is concealed inside that dragon semblance: an animal more similar to those we are at home with, a living presence less distant from us than it seems. . . .

Then there are other spiky crests under the chin; on

the neck there are two round white plates like a hearing
aid; a number of accessories and sundries, trimmings,
and defensive garnishings, a sample case of forms available in the animal kingdom and perhaps also in other
kingdoms—too much stuff for one animal to bear.
What's the use of it? Does it serve to disguise someone
watching us from in there?

The forelegs, with five fingers, would suggest talons
rather than hands if they were not attached to actual
arms, muscular and well shaped; but the hind legs are
different, long and flabby, with fingers like vegetable
propagations. The animal as a whole, however, even
from the depths of his resigned, motionless torpor,
conveys an image of strength.

At the glass case of the *Iguana iguana* Mr. Palomar
has stopped, after having contemplated the case with
ten little iguanas clinging one to another, constantly
shifting position with agile movements of elbows and
knees, all stretching in a lengthwise direction: the skin
a brilliant green, with a copper-colored dot in the place
of gills, a crested white beard, pale eyes wide around
the black pupil. Then the savanna monitor, which hides
in sand its identical color; the Teju or Tupinambis, yellowish black, almost an alligator; the giant African
Cordilo, with thick, pointed scales like fur or leaves,
the color of the desert, so concentrated in its determi-
nation to exclude itself from the world that it coils in a
circle, curling its tail against its head. The gray-green
upper shell and the white underneath of a turtle immersed in the water of a transparent tank seem soft,
fleshy; the pointed head emerges as if from a high
collar.

Life in the reptile house appears a squandering of forms without style and without plan, where all is possible, and animals and plants and rocks exchange scales, quills, concretions. But among the infinite possible combinations, only some—perhaps actually the most incredible—become fixed, resist the flux that undoes them and mixes and reshapes; and immediately each of these forms becomes the center of a world, separated forever from the others, as here in the row of glass case-cages of the zoo; and in this finite number of ways of being, each identified in a monstrosity of its own, and a necessity and beauty of its own, lies order, the sole order recognizable in the world. The iguana room of the Jardin des Plantes, with its illuminated cases, where dozing reptiles are hidden among branches and rocks and sand of the forest or the desert of their origin, reflects the order of the world, whether it be the reflection on earth of the sky of ideas or the external manifestation of the secret of the nature of creation, of the norm concealed in the depths of that which exists.

Is it this atmosphere, more than the reptiles in themselves, that obscurely attracts Mr. Palomar? A damp, soft warmth soaks the air like a sponge; a sharp stink, heavy, rotten, forces him to hold his breath; shadow and light lie stagnant in a motionless mixture of days and nights: are these the sensations of a man who peers out beyond the human? Beyond the glass of every cage there is the world as it was before man, or as it will be, to show that the world of man is not eternal and is not unique. Is it to realize this with his own eyes that Mr. Palomar reviews these stalls where pytho s sleep, boas, bamboo rattlesnakes, the tree adder of the Bermudas?

The Silences
of Mr. Palomar

MR. PALOMAR'S
JOURNEYS

The sand garden

A little courtyard covered with a white sand, thick-grained, almost gravel, raked in straight, parallel furrows or in concentric circles, around five irregular groups of stones or low boulders. This is one of the most famous monuments of Japanese civilization, the garden of rocks and sand of the Ryoanji of Kyoto, the image typical of that contemplation of the absolute to be achieved with the simplest means and without recourse to concepts capable of verbal expression, according to the teaching of the Zen monks, the most spiritual of Buddhist sects.

The rectangular enclosure of colorless sand is flanked on three sides by walls surmounted by tiles, beyond which is the green of trees. On the fourth side is a wooden platform, of steps, where the public can file by or linger and sit down. "Absorbed in this scene," explains the pamphlet offered to visitors, in Japanese and in English, signed by the abbot of the temple, "we, who think of ourselves as relative, are filled with serene wonder as we intuit Absolute Self, and our stained minds are purified."

Mr. Palomar is prepared to accept this advice on faith,

and he sits on the steps, observes the rocks one by one, follows the undulations of the white sand, allows the undefinable harmony that links the elements of the picture gradually to pervade him.

Or, rather, he tries to imagine all these things as they would be felt by someone who could concentrate on looking at the Zen garden in solitude and silence. Because—we had forgotten to say—Mr. Palomar is crammed on the platform in the midst of hundreds of visitors, who jostle him on every side; camera lenses and movie cameras force their way past the elbows, knees, ears of the crowd, to frame the rocks and the sand from every angle, illuminated by natural light or by flashbulbs. Swarms of feet in wool socks step over him (shoes, as always in Japan, are left at the entrance); numerous offspring are thrust to the front row by pedagogical parents; clumps of uniformed students shove one another, eager only to conclude as quickly as possible this school outing to the famous monument; earnest visitors nodding their heads rhythmically check and make sure that everything written in the guidebook corresponds to reality and that everything seen in reality is also mentioned in the guide.

"We can view the garden as a group of mountainous islands in a great ocean, or as mountain tops rising above a sea of clouds. We can see it as a picture framed by the ancient mud walls, or we can forget the frame as we sense the truth of this sea stretching out boundlessly."

These "instructions for use" are contained in the leaflet, and to Mr. Palomar they seem perfectly plausible and immediately applicable, without effort, provided one is really sure of having a personality to shed, of looking at the world from inside an ego that can be dissolved, to become only a gaze. But it is precisely this outset that demands an effort of supplementary imagination, very difficult to muster when one's ego is glued into a solid crowd looking through its thousand eyes and walking on its thousand feet along the established itinerary of the tourist visit.

Must the conclusion be that the Zen mental techniques for achieving extreme humility, detachment from all possessiveness and pride, require as their necessary background aristocratic privilege, and assume an individualism with so much space and so much time around it, the horizons of a solitude free of anguish?

But this conclusion, which leads to the familiar lament over a paradise lost in the spread of mass civilization, sounds too facile for Mr. Palomar. He prefers to take a more difficult path, to try to grasp what the Zen garden can give him, looking at it in the only situation in which it can be looked at today, craning his neck among other necks.

What does he see? He sees the human race in the era of great numbers, which extends in a crowd, leveled but still made up of distinct individualities like the sea of grains of sand that submerges the surface of the world. . . . He sees that the world, nevertheless, continues to turn the boulder-backs of its nature indifferent to the fate of mankind, its hard substance that cannot be reduced to human assimilation. . . . He sees the forms in which the assembled human sand tends to arrange itself along lines of movement, patterns that combine regularity and fluidity like the rectilinear or circular

tracks of a rake. . . . And between mankind-sand and
world-boulder there is a sense of possible harmony, as
if between two nonhomogeneous harmonies: that of the
nonhuman in a balance of forces that seems not to correspond to any pattern, and that of human structures,
which aspires to the rationality of a geometrical or mu-
sical composition, never definitive. . . .

Serpents and skulls

In Mexico, Mr. Palomar is visiting the ruins of Tula, ancient capital of the Toltecs. A Mexican friend accompanies him, an impassioned and eloquent expert on pre-Columbian civilizations, who tells him beautiful legends about Quetzalcoatl. Before becoming a god, Quetzalcoatl was a king, with his palace here in Tula; a line of lopped-off columns remains, around an impluvium, a bit like a palace of ancient Rome.

The temple of the Morning Star is a step pyramid. At the top stand four cylindrical caryatids, known as "Atlases," who represent the god Quetzalcoatl as the Morning Star (through a butterfly they bear on their back, symbol of the star), and four carved columns, which represent the Plumed Serpent, the same god in animal form.

All this has to be taken on faith; for that matter, it would be hard to demonstrate the opposite. In Mexican archeology every statue, every object, every detail of a bas-relief stands for something that stands for something else that stands, in turn, for yet another something. An animal stands for a god who stands for a star that stands for an element or a human quality, and so on. We are in the world of pictographic writing; the ancient Mexicans, to write, drew pictures, and even when they were drawing it was as if they were writing: every picture seems a rebus to be deciphered. Even the most abstract, geometric friezes on the wall of a temple can be interpreted as arrows if you see a motive of broken lines, or you can read a numerical sequence, depending on the way the key pattern is repeated. Here in Tula the reliefs depict stylized animal forms: jaguars, coyotes. Mr. Palomar's Mexican friend pauses at each stone, transforms it into a cosmic tale, an allegory, a moral reflection.

A group of schoolchildren moves among the ruins: stocky boys with the features of the Indios, descendants perhaps of the builders of these temples, wearing plain white uniforms, like boy scouts', with blue neckerchiefs. The boys are led by a teacher not much taller than they are and only a little more adult, with the same round, dark, impassive face. They climb the steep steps of the pyramid, stop beneath the columns; the teacher tells what civilization they belong to, what century, what stone they are carved from, then concludes, "We don't know what they mean," and the group follows him down the steps. At each statue, each figure carved in a relief or on a column, the teacher supplies some facts and then invariably adds, "We don't know what it means."

Here is a *chac-mool*, a very popular kind of statue: a human figure, half reclining, holds a tray; on this tray— the experts are unanimous in saying—the bleeding hearts of the victims of human sacrifice were presented. These statues in and of themselves could also be seen as good-natured, rough-hewn puppets; but every time Mr. Palomar sees one he cannot help shuddering.

The line of schoolboys passes. And the teacher is saying, "*Esto es un chac-mool. No se sabe lo que quiere decir.*" ("This is a *chac-mool*. We don't know what it means.") And he moves on.

Though Mr. Palomar continues to follow the explanation of his friend acting as guide, he always ends up crossing the path of the schoolboys and overhearing the teacher's words. He is fascinated by his friend's wealth of mythological references: the play of interpretation and allegorical reading has always seemed to him a supreme exercise of the mind. But he feels attracted also by the opposite attitude of the schoolteacher: what had at first seemed only a brisk lack of interest is being revealed to him as a scholarly and pedagogical position, a methodological choice by this serious and conscientious young man, a rule from which he will not swerve. A stone, a figure, a sign, a word reaching us isolated from its context is only that stone, figure, sign, or word: we can try to define them, to describe them as they are, and no more than that; whether, beside the face they show us, they also have a hidden face, is not for us to know. The refusal to comprehend more than what the stones show us is perhaps the only way to evince respect for their secret; trying to guess is a presumption, a betrayal of that true, lost meaning.

Behind the pyramid is a passage or communication trench between two walls, one of packed earth, the other of carved stone: the Wall of the Serpents. It is perhaps the most beautiful piece in Tula; in the relief-frieze there is a sequence of serpents, each holding a human skull in its open jaws, as if it were about to devour it.

The boys go by. The teacher says: "This is the Wall of the Serpents. Each serpent has a skull in its mouth. We don't know what they mean."

Mr. Palomar's friend cannot contain himself: "Yes, we do! It's the continuity of life and death; the serpents are life, the skulls are death. Life is life because it bears death with it, and death is death because there is no life without death. . . ."

The boys listen, mouths agape, black eyes dazed. Mr. Palomar thinks that every translation requires another translation, and so on. He asks himself: "What did death, life, continuity, passage mean for the ancient Toltecs? And what can they mean today for these boys? And for me?" Yet he knows he could never suppress in himself the need to translate, to move from one language to another, from concrete figures to abstract words, to weave and reweave a network of analogies. Not to interpret is impossible, as refraining from thinking is impossible.

Once the school group has disappeared around a corner, the stubborn voice of the little teacher resumes: "*No es verdad*, it is not true, what that *señor* said. We don't know what they mean."

The odd slipper

While traveling in an Eastern country, Mr. Palomar bought a pair of slippers in a bazaar. Returning home, he tries to put them on; he realizes that one slipper is wider than the other and will not stay on his foot. He recalls the old vendor crouched on his heels in a niche of the bazaar in front of a pile of slippers of every size, at random; he sees the man as he rummages in the pile to find a slipper suited to the customer's foot, has him try it on, then starts rummaging again to hand him the presumed mate, which Mr. Palomar accepts without trying it on.

"Perhaps now," Mr. Palomar thinks, "another man is walking around that country with a mismated pair of slippers." And he sees a slender shadow moving over the desert with a limp, a slipper falling off his foot at every step or else, too tight, imprisoning a twisted foot. "Perhaps he, too, is thinking of me, at this moment, hoping to run into me and make the trade. The relationship binding us is more concrete and clear than many of the relationships established between human beings. And yet we will never meet." He decides to go on wearing these odd slippers out of solidarity with his unknown companion in misfortune, to keep alive this complementary relationship that is so rare, this mirroring of limping steps from one continent to another.

He lingers over this image, but he knows it does not correspond to the truth. An avalanche of slippers, sewn on an assembly line, comes periodically to top up the old merchant's pile in that bazaar. At the bottom of the pile there will always remain two odd slippers, but until the old merchant exhausts his supply (and perhaps he will never exhaust it, and after his death the shop with all its merchandise will pass to his heirs and to the heirs of his heirs), it will suffice to search in the pile and one slipper will always be found to match another slipper. A mistake can occur only with an absent-minded customer like himself, but centuries can go by before the consequences of this mistake affect another visitor to that ancient bazaar. Every process of disintegration in the order of the world is irreversible; the effects, however, are hidden and delayed by the dust cloud of the big numbers, which contains virtually limitless possibilities of new symmetries, combinations, pairings.

But what if his mistake had simply erased an earlier mistake? What if his absent-mindedness had been the bearer not of disorder but of order? "Perhaps the merchant knew what he was doing," Mr. Palomar thinks. "In giving me that mismated slipper, he was righting a disparity that had been hidden for centuries in that pile of slippers, handed down from generation to generation in that bazaar."

The unknown companion was limping perhaps in another time, the symmetry of their steps responded not only from one continent to another but over a distance of centuries. This does not make Mr. Palomar feel less solidarity with him. He goes on shuffling awkwardly, to afford relief to his shadow.

MR. PALOMAR
IN SOCIETY

On biting the tongue

In a time and in a country where everyone goes out of his way to announce opinions or hand down judgments, Mr. Palomar has made a habit of biting his tongue three times before asserting anything. After the third bite, if he is still convinced of what he was going to say, he says it. If not, he keeps his mouth shut. In fact, he spends whole weeks, months in silence.

Good opportunities for keeping quiet are never in short supply, but there are also rare occasions when Mr. Palomar regrets not having said something he could have said at the right moment. He realizes that events have confirmed what he was thinking and that if he had expressed his thoughts at the time, he would have had a positive influence, however slight, on what then ensued. In these cases his spirit is torn between self-satisfaction for having seen things properly and a sense of guilt because of his excessive reserve. Both feelings are so strong that he is tempted to put them into words; but after having bitten his tongue three times—or, rather, six—he is convinced he has no cause either for pride or for remorse.

Having had the correct view is nothing meritorious:

statistically, it is almost inevitable that among the many cockeyed, confused, or banal ideas that come into his mind, there should also be some perspicacious ideas, even ideas of genius; and since they occurred to him, they can surely have occurred to somebody else as well.

Whether he should refrain from expressing his idea is more debatable. In times of general silence, conforming to the silence of the majority is certainly wrong. In times when everybody says too much, the important thing is not merely to say what is right, which in any event would be engulfed in the flood of words, but to say it on the basis of premises and consequences, so that what is said acquires the maximum value. But, then, if the value of a single affirmation lies in the continuity and coherence of the discourse in which it is uttered, the only possible choice is between speaking continuously or never speaking at all. In the first case Mr. Palomar would reveal that his thinking does not proceed in a straight line but zigzags its way through vacillations, denials, corrections, in whose midst the rightness of that affirmation of his would be lost. As for the other alternative, it implies an art of keeping silent even more difficult than the art of speaking.

In fact, silence can also be considered a kind of speech, since it is a rejection of the use to which others put words; but the meaning of this silence-speech lies in its interruptions in what is, from time to time, actually said, giving a meaning to what is unsaid.

Or rather: a silence can serve to dismiss certain words or else to hold them in reserve for use on a better occasion. Just as a word spoken now can save a hundred words tomorrow or else can necessitate the saying of

another thousand. "Every time I bite my tongue,"
Mr. Palomar concludes mentally, "I must think not only
of what I am about to say or not say, but also of everything that, whether I say it or do not say it, will be said
or not said by me or by others." Having formulated
this thought, he bites his tongue and remains silent.

On getting angry at the young

In a time when young people's impatience with the old and old people's impatience with the young have reached their peak, when the old do nothing but store up arguments with which to tell the young finally what they deserve and when the young are waiting only for these occasions in order to show the old that they understand nothing, Mr. Palomar is unable to utter a word. If he sometimes tries to speak up, he realizes that all are too intent on the theses they are defending to pay any attention to what he is trying to clarify to himself.

The fact is that he would like not so much to affirm a truth of his own as to ask questions, and he realizes that no one wants to abandon the train of his own discourse to answer questions that, coming from another discourse, would necessitate rethinking the same things with other words, perhaps ending up on strange ground, far from safe paths. Or else he would like others to ask him questions; but he, too, would want only certain questions and not others: the ones he would answer by saying the things he feels he can say but could say only if someone asked him to say them. In any event, nobody has the slightest idea of asking him anything.

In this situation Mr. Palomar confines himself to brooding privately on the difficulty of speaking to the young.

He thinks: "The difficulty lies in the fact that between us and them there is an unbridgeable gap. Something has happened between our generation and theirs, a continuity of experience has been broken: we no longer have any common reference points."

Then he thinks: "No, the difficulty lies in the fact that every time I am about to reproach or criticize or exhort or advise them, I think that as a young man I also attracted reproaches, criticism, exhortation, advice of the same sort, and I never listened to any of it. Times were different and as a result there were many differences in behavior, language, customs; but my mental processes then were not very different from theirs today. So I have no authority to speak."

Mr. Palomar vacillates at length between these two views of the question. Then he decides: "There is no contradiction between the two positions. The break between the generations derives from the impossibility of transmitting experience, of saving others from making the mistakes we have already made. The real distance between two generations is created by the elements they have in common, which require the cyclical repetition of the same experiences, as in the biologically inherited behavior of animal species. The differences between us and them, on the contrary, are the result of the irreversible changes that every period evolves; and these differences are the result of the historical legacy that we have handed on to them, the true legacy for which we are responsible, even if unconsciously sometimes. This is why we have nothing to teach: we can exert no influence on what most resembles our own experience; in what bears our own imprint we are unable to recognize ourselves."

The model of models

In Mr. Palomar's life there was a period when his rule was this: first, to construct in his mind a model, the most perfect, logical, geometrical model possible; second, to see if the model was suited to the practical situations observed in experience; third, to make the corrections necessary for model and reality to coincide. This procedure, developed by physicists and astronomers, who investigate the structure of matter and of the universe, seemed to Mr. Palomar the only way to tackle the most entangled human problems, such as those involving society and the art of government. He had to bear in mind the shapeless and senseless reality of human society, with all its monstrosities and disasters, and, at the same time, a model of the perfect social organism, designed with neatly drawn lines, straight or circular or elliptical, parallelograms of forms, diagrams with abscissas and ordinates.

To construct a model—as Mr. Palomar was aware—you have to start with something; that is, you have to have principles, from which, by deduction, you develop your own line of reasoning. These principles—also known as axioms or postulates—are not something

you select; you have them already, because if you did
not have them, you could not even begin thinking. So
Mr. Palomar also had some, but, since he was neither
a mathematician nor a logician, he did not bother to
define them. Deduction, in any case, was one of his
favorite activities, because he could devote himself to it
in silence and alone, without special equipment, at any
place and moment, seated in his armchair or strolling.
Induction, on the contrary, was something he did not
really trust, perhaps because he thought his experiences
vague and incomplete. The construction of a model,
therefore, was for him a miracle of equilibrium between
principles (left in shadow) and experience (elusive), but
the result should be more substantial than either. In a
well-made model, in fact, every detail must be conditioned by the others, so that everything holds together
in absolute coherence, as in a mechanism where if one
gear jams, everything jams. A model is by definition
that in which nothing has to be changed, that which
works perfectly; whereas reality, as we see clearly, does
not work and constantly falls to pieces; so we must
force it, more or less roughly, to assume the form of
the model.

For a long time Mr. Palomar made an effort to achieve
such impassiveness and detachment that what counted
was only the serene harmony of the lines of the pattern:
all the lacerations and contortions and compressions that
human reality has to undergo to conform to the model
were to be considered transitory, irrelevant accidents.
But if for a moment he stopped gazing at the harmonious geometrical design drawn in the heaven of ideal
models, a human landscape leaped to his eye where

monstrosities and disasters had not vanished at all and
the lines of the design seemed distorted and twisted.

A delicate job of adjustment was then required, making
gradual corrections in the model so it would approach
a possible reality, and in reality to make it approach the
model. In fact, the degree of pliability in human nature
is not unlimited, as he first believed; and at the same
time, even the most rigid model can show some unex-
pected elasticity. In other words, if the model does not
succeed in transforming reality, reality must succeed in
transforming the model.

Mr. Palomar's rule had gradually been changing: now
he needed a great variety of models, whose elements
could be combined in order to arrive at the one that
would best fit reality, a reality that, for its own part,
was always made up of many different realities, in time
and in space.

Throughout this period, Mr. Palomar did not develop models himself or try to apply those already developed: he confined himself to imagining a right use
of the right models to bridge the gap that he saw yawn-
ing, ever wider, between reality and principles. In other
words, the way in which models could be managed and
manipulated was not his responsibility, nor was it in
his power to intervene. People who concerned themselves with these things were usually quite different from
him. They judged the models' functionality by other
criteria: as instruments of power especially, rather than
according to principles or to consequences. This attitude was fairly natural, since what the models seek to
model is basically always a system of power; but if the
efficacy of the system is measured by its invulnerability

and capacity to last, the model becomes a kind of fortress whose thick walls conceal what is outside. Mr. Palomar, who from powers and counterpowers expects always the worst, was finally convinced that what really counts is what happens *despite* them: the form that society is assuming slowly, silently, anonymously, in people's habits, their way of thinking and acting, their scale of values. If this is how things stand, the model of models Mr. Palomar dreams of must serve to achieve transparent models, diaphanous, fine as cobwebs, or perhaps even to dissolve models, or indeed to dissolve itself.

At this point the only thing Mr. Palomar can do is erase from his mind all models and models of models. Having taken this step, he is face to face with reality—hard to master and impossible to make uniform—as he utters his "yes"es and his "no"s, his "but"s. To do this, it is better for the mind to remain cleared, furnished only by the memory of fragments of experience and of principles implied but not demonstrable. This is not a line of conduct from which he can derive special satisfactions, but it is the only one that proves practicable for him.

As long as it is a matter of demonstrating the ills of society and the abuses of those who abuse, he has no hesitations (except the fear that, if they are talked about too much, even the most just propositions can sound repetitive, obvious, tired). He finds it more difficult to say something about the remedies, because first he would like to make sure that they do not cause worse ills and abuses, and that wisely planned by enlightened reformers, they can be put into practice without harm by their successors: foolish perhaps, perhaps frauds, perhaps frauds and foolish at once.

He has only to expound these fine thoughts in a systematic form, but a scruple restrains him: what if all this becomes a model? And so he prefers to keep his convictions in the fluid state, check them instance by instance, and make them the implicit rule of his own everyday behavior, in doing or not doing, in choosing or rejecting, in speaking or in remaining silent.

THE MEDITATIONS OF
MR. PALOMAR

The world looks at the world

After a series of intellectual misadventures not worth
recalling, Mr. Palomar has decided that his chief activ-
ity will be looking at things from the outside. A bit
nearsighted, absent-minded, introverted, he does not
seem to belong temperamentally to that human type
generally called an observer. And yet it has always happened that certain things—a stone wall, a seashell, a
leaf, a teapot—present themselves to him as if asking
him for minute and prolonged attention: he starts observing them almost unawares, and his gaze begins to
run over all the details and is then unable to detach
itself. Mr. Palomar has decided that from now on he
will redouble his attention: first, by not allowing these
summons to escape him as they arrive from things; second, by attributing to the observer's operation the importance it deserves.

At this point he faces his first critical moment: sure
that from now on the world will reveal to him an infinite wealth of things, Mr. Palomar tries staring at
everything that comes within eyeshot; he feels no pleasure, and he stops. A second phase follows, in which
he is convinced that only some things are to be looked

at, others not, and he must go and seek the right ones. To do this, he has to face each time problems of selection, exclusion, hierarchies of preference; he soon realizes he is spoiling everything, as always when he involves his own ego and all the problems he has with his own ego.

But how can you look at something and set your own ego aside? Whose eyes are doing the looking? As a rule, you think of the ego as one who is peering out of your own eyes as if leaning on a window sill, looking at the world stretching out before him in all its immensity. So, then: a window looks out on the world. The world is out there; and in here, what do we have? The world still—what else could there be? With a little effort of concentration, Mr. Palomar manages to shift the world from in front of him and set it on the sill, looking out. Now, beyond the window, what do we have? The world is also there, and for the occasion has been split into a looking world and a world looked at. And what about him, also known as "I," namely Mr. Palomar? Is he not a piece of the world that is looking at another piece of the world? Or else, given that there is world that side of the window and world this side, perhaps the "I," the ego, is simply the window through which the world looks at the world. To look at itself the world needs the eyes (and the eyeglasses) of Mr. Palomar.

So, from now on Mr. Palomar will look at things from outside and not from inside. But this is not enough: he will look at them with a gaze that comes from outside, not inside, himself. He tries to perform the experiment at once: now it is not he who is looking; it is the world of outside that is looking outside. Having established this, he casts his gaze around, expecting a general transfiguration. No such thing. The usual quotidian grayness surrounds him. Everything has to be rethought from the beginning. Having the outside look outside is not enough: the trajectory must start from the looked-at thing, linking it with the thing that looks.

From the mute distance of things a sign must come, a summons, a wink: one thing detaches itself from the other things with the intention of signifying something . . . what? Itself, a thing is happy to be looked at by other things only when it is convinced that it signifies itself and nothing else, amid things that signify themselves and nothing else.

Opportunities of this kind are not frequent, to be sure; but sooner or later they will have to arise: it is enough to wait for one of those lucky coincidences to occur when the world wants to look and be looked at in the same instant and Mr. Palomar happens to be going by. Or, rather, Mr. Palomar does not even have to wait, because these things happen only when you are not awaiting them.

The universe as mirror

Mr. Palomar suffers greatly because of his difficulty in establishing relations with his fellow man. He envies people who have the gift of always finding the right thing to say, the right greeting for everyone; people who are at ease with anyone they happen to encounter and put others at their ease; who move easily among people and immediately understand when they must defend themselves and keep their distance or when they can win trust and affection; who give their best in their relations with others and make others want to give their best; who know at once how to evaluate a person with regard to themselves and on an absolute scale.

"These gifts," Mr. Palomar thinks with the regret of the man who lacks them, "are granted to those who live in harmony with the world. It is natural for them to establish an accord not only with people but also with things, places, situations, occasions, with the course of the constellations in the firmament, with the aggregation of atoms in molecules. That avalanche of simultaneous events that we call the universe does not overwhelm the lucky individual who can slip through the finest interstices among the infinite combinations, permutations, chains of consequences, avoiding the paths of the murderous meteorites and catching only the beneficent rays. To the man who is the friend of the universe, the universe is a friend. If only," Mr. Palomar sighs, "I could be like that!"

He decides to try to imitate such people. All his efforts, from now on, will be directed toward achieving a harmony both with the human race, his neighbor, and with the most distant spiral of the system of the galaxies. To begin with, since he has too many problems with his neighbor, Mr. Palomar will try to improve his relations with the universe. He avoids and reduces to a minimum his association with his similars; he grows accustomed to making his mind a blank, expelling all indiscreet presences; he observes the sky on starry nights; he reads books on astronomy; he becomes familiar with the notion of sidereal spaces until this becomes a permanent piece in his mental furniture. Then he tries to make his thoughts retain simultaneously the nearest things and the farthest: when he lights his pipe he is intent on the flame of the match that at his next puff should allow itself to be drawn to the bottom of the bowl, initiating the slow transformation of shreds of tobacco into embers; but this attention must not make him forget even for a moment the explosion of a supernova taking place in the Large Magellanic Cloud at this same instant (that is to say, a few million years ago). The idea that everything in the universe is connected and corresponds never leaves him: a variation in the brightness of the Crab nebula or the condensation of a globular mass in Andromeda cannot help having some influence on the functioning of his record player or on the freshness of the watercress leaves in his salad bowl.

When he is convinced that he has precisely outlined

his own place in the midst of the silent expanse of things
floating in the void, amid the dust cloud of present or
possible events that hovers in space and time, Mr. Palomar decides the moment has come to apply this cosmic
wisdom to relations with his fellows. He hastens to return to society, renews acquaintances, friendships, business associations; he subjects his ties and affections to a
careful examination of conscience. He expects to see,
extending before him, a human landscape that is finally
distinct, clear, without mists, where he will be able to
move with precise and confident gestures. Is this what
happens? Not at all. He starts by becoming embroiled
in a muddle of misunderstandings, hesitations, com-
promises, blunders; the most futile matters stir up anguish, the most serious lose their point; everything he
says or does proves clumsy, jarring, irresolute. What is
it that does not work?

This: contemplating the stars he has become accustomed to considering himself an anonymous and incor-
poreal dot, almost forgetting that he exists; to deal now
with human beings, he cannot help involving himself,
and he no longer knows where his self is to be found.
In dealing with another person everyone should know
where to place himself with regard to that person, should
be sure of the reaction the other's presence inspires—
dislike or attraction, dominion or subjugation, disciple-
ship or mastery, performance as actor or as spectator—
and on the basis of it and its counterreaction he should
then establish the rules of the game to be applied in
their play, the moves and countermoves to be made.
But for all this, even before he starts observing the others, he should know well who he is himself. Knowl-

edge of one's fellow has this special aspect: it passes necessarily through knowledge of oneself; and this is precisely what Mr. Palomar is lacking. Not only knowledge is needed, but also comprehension, agreement with one's own means and ends and impulses, which implies a mastery over one's own inclinations and actions that will control and direct them but not coerce or stifle them. The people he admires for the rightness and naturalness of their every word and every action are not only at peace with the universe but, first of all, at peace with themselves. Mr. Palomar, who does not love himself, has always taken care not to encounter himself face to face; this is why he preferred to take refuge among the galaxies; now he understands that he should have begun by finding an inner peace. The universe can perhaps go tranquilly about its business; he surely cannot.

The only way still open to him is self-knowledge; from now on he will explore his own inner geography, he will draw the diagram of the moods of his spirit, he will derive from it formulas and theories, he will train his telescope on the orbits traced by the course of his life rather than on those of the constellations. "We can know nothing about what is outside us if we overlook ourselves," he thinks now. "The universe is the mirror in which we can contemplate only what we have learned to know in ourselves."

And thus this new phase of his itinerary in search of wisdom is also achieved. Finally his gaze can rove freely inside himself. What will he see? Will his inner world seem to him an immense, calm rotation of a luminous spiral? Will he see stars and planets navigating in silence

on the parabolas and ellipses that determine character
and destiny? Will he contemplate a sphere of infinite
circumference that has the ego as its center and its center in every point?

He opens his eyes. What appears to his gaze is something he seems to have seen already, every day: streets
full of people, hurrying, elbowing their way ahead,
without looking one another in the face, among high
walls, sharp and peeling. In the background, the starry
sky scatters intermittent flashes like a stalled mechanism, which jerks and creaks in all its unoiled joints,
outposts of an endangered universe, twisted, restless as
he is.

Learning to be dead

Mr. Palomar decides that from now on he will act as if he were dead, to see how the world gets along without him. For some while he has realized that things between him and the world are no longer proceeding as they used to; before, they seemed to expect something of each other, he and the world; now he no longer recalls what there was to expect, good or bad, or why this expectation kept him in a perpetually agitated, anxious state.

So now Mr. Palomar should feel a sensation of relief, no longer having to wonder what the world has in store for him; and there should be relief also for the world, which no longer has to bother about him. But it is the very expectation of enjoying this calm that makes Mr. Palomar anxious.

In other words, being dead is less easy than it might seem. First of all, you must not confuse being dead with not being, a condition that occupies the vast expanse of time before birth, apparently symmetrical with the other, equally vast expanse that follows death. In fact, before birth we are part of the infinite possibilities that may or may not be fulfilled; whereas, once dead, we cannot fulfill ourselves either in the past (to which we now belong entirely but on which we can no longer have any influence) or in the future (which, even if influenced by us, remains forbidden to us). Mr. Palomar's case is really simpler, since his capacity for having an influence on anything or anybody has always been negligible: the world can very well do without him, and he can consider himself dead quite serenely, without even altering his habits. The problem is not the change in what he does but in what he is, or, more specifically, in what he is as far as the world is concerned. Before, by "world" he meant the world plus himself; now it is a question of himself plus the world minus him.

Does the world minus him mean an end to anxiety? A world in which things happen independently of his presence and his reactions, following a law of their own or a necessity or rationale that does not involve him? The wave strikes the cliff and hollows out the rock, another wave arrives, another, and still another; whether he is or is not, everything goes on happening. The relief in being dead should be this: having eliminated that patch of uneasiness that is our presence, the only thing that matters is the extension and succession of things under the sun, in their impassive serenity. All is calm or tends toward calm, even hurricanes, earthquakes, the eruption of volcanoes. But was this not the earlier world, when he was in it? When every storm bore within itself the peace of afterward, prepared the moment when all the waves would have struck the shore, and the wind would have spent its force? Perhaps being dead is passing into the ocean of the waves that remain waves forever, so it is futile to wait for the sea to become calm.

The gaze of the dead is always a bit deprecatory. Places, situations, occasions are more or less what one already knew, and recognizing them always affords a certain satisfaction; but at the same time many variations, large and small, become noticeable. In and of themselves they might be acceptable, too, if they corresponded to a logical, coherent process; but instead they prove arbitrary and irregular, and this is irksome, especially because one is always tempted to intervene and make the correction that seems necessary, and, being dead, one cannot do it. Hence an attitude of reluctance, almost of embarrassment, but at the same time of smugness, the attitude of one who knows that what counts is his own past experience and there is no point in attaching too much importance to all the rest. Then a dominant feeling is quick to arise and impose itself on every thought: it is the relief of knowing that all those problems are other people's problems, their business. The dead should no longer give a damn about anything, because it is not up to them to think about it any more; and even if that may seem immoral, it is in this irresponsibility that the dead find their gaiety.

The more Mr. Palomar's spiritual condition approaches the one here described, the more the idea of being dead seems natural to him. To be sure, he has not yet found the sublime detachment he thought was usual with the dead, or a reason that surpasses all explanation, or an emergence from his own confines as if he were emerging from a tunnel that opens out into other dimensions. At times he has the illusion of being freed at least from the impatience he has felt all his life at seeing others do everything wrong and in thinking that in their place he would also do it wrong but would at least be aware of his errors. But he is not really free of this impatience, and he realizes that his intolerance of others' mistakes and his own will be perpetuated along with those mistakes, which no death can erase. So he might as well get used to it: for Mr. Palomar being dead means resigning himself to remaining the same in a definitive state, which he can no longer hope to change.

Mr. Palomar does not underestimate the advantages that the condition of being alive can have over that of being dead: not as regards the future, where risks are always very great and benefits can be of short duration, but in the sense of the possibility of improving the form of one's own past. (Unless one is already fully satisfied with one's own past, a situation too uninteresting to make it worth investigating.) A person's life consists of a collection of events, the last of which could also change the meaning of the whole, not because it counts more than the previous ones but because once they are included in a life, events are arranged in an order that is not chronological but, rather, corresponds to an inner architecture. A person, for example, reads in adulthood a book that is important for him, and it makes him say, "How could I have lived without having read it!," and also, "What a pity I did not read it in my youth!" Well, these statements do not have much meaning, especially the second, because after he has read that book, his whole life becomes the life of a person who has read that book, and it is of little importance whether he read it early or late, because now his life before that reading also assumes a form shaped by that reading.

This is the most difficult step in learning how to be dead: to become convinced that your own life is a closed whole, all in the past, to which you can add nothing and can alter none of the relationships among the various elements. Of course, those who go on living can, according to their shifting experience, introduce changes in the lives of the dead, too, giving form to what had none or what seemed to have a different form: recognizing, for example, a just rebel in someone who had been vituperated for his lawless actions, celebrating a poet or a prophet in one who had felt doomed to neurosis or delirium. But these are changes that matter mostly to the living. It is unlikely that they, the dead, will profit by them. Each individual is made up of what he has lived and the way he lived it, and no one can take this away from him. Anyone who has lived in suffering is always made of that suffering; if they try to take it away from him, he is no longer himself.

Therefore, Mr. Palomar prepares to become a grouchy dead man, reluctant to submit to the sentence to remain exactly as he is; but he is unwilling to give up anything of himself, even if it is a burden.

Of course, it is also possible to rely on those devices that guarantee survival of at least a part of the self in posterity. These views can be divided into two broad categories: the biological mechanism, which allows leaving to descendants that part of the self known as the genetic heritage; and the historical mechanism, which grants a continuance in the memory and language of those who go on living and inherit that portion, large or small, of experience that even the most inept man gathers and stores up. These mechanisms can also be seen as a single one, considering the succession of generations like the stages in the life of a single person, which goes on for centuries and millennia; but this is simply a postponement of the problem, from one's own, individual death to the extinction of the human race, however late this may occur.

Thinking of his own death, Mr. Palomar already thinks of that of the last survivors of the human species or of its derivations or heirs: on the terrestrial globe, devastated and deserted, explorers from another planet land; they decipher the clues recorded in the hieroglyphics of the pyramids and in the punched cards of the electronic calculators; the memory of the human race is reborn from its ashes and is spread through the inhabited zones of the universe. And so, after one postponement or another, the moment comes when it is time to wear out and be extinguished in an empty sky, when the last material evidence of the memory of living will degenerate in a flash of heat, or will crystallize its atoms in the chill of an immobile order.

"If time has to end, it can be described, instant by instant," Mr. Palomar thinks, "and each instant, when described, expands so that its end can no longer be seen." He decides that he will set himself to describing every instant of his life, and until he has described them all he will no longer think of being dead. At that moment he dies.

Index

The numbers 1, 2, 3 that mark the titles of the index, whether they are in the first, second, or third position, besides having a purely ordinal value, correspond also to three thematic areas, three kinds of experience and inquiry that, in varying proportions, are present in every part of the book.

Those marked "1" generally correspond to a visual experience, whose object is almost always some natural form; the text tends to the descriptive.

Those marked "2" contain elements that are anthropological, or cultural in the broad sense; and the experience involves, besides visual data, also language, meaning, symbols. The text tends to take the form of a story.

Those marked "3" involve more speculative experience, concerning the cosmos, time, infinity, the relationship between the self and the world, the dimensions of the mind. From description and narrative we move into meditation.

Printed in the USA
CPSIA information can be obtained
at www.ICGtesting.com
LVHW031921050924
790233LV00007B/429

9 780156 627801